'The facility for language remains unparalleled . . . Writing this rich should be cherished . . . *No Country For Old Men* is a severed head and shoulders over anything else written in America this year'

Independent on Sunday

'No one has McCarthy's ear for regional talk, nor eye for details of place. The writing transforms a standard western good-guy bad-guy plot into serious literature . . . The book inspires discussion and reading groups will surely have vigorous responses to it . . . McCarthy's oeuvre can be seen as the ongoing study of a burning American rage, and how common that rage has become'

Annie Proulx, *Guardian* Book of the Week

'Where his earlier books employ an almost lingering style, *No Country For Old Men* races on as fast and relentlessly as the nemesis that bears down upon his characters . . . [an] utterly absorbing, chilling tale . . . [Chigurh is] one of the most sinister characters in modern American fiction . . . McCarthy's economy of language is stunning, characters defined by a line of conversation, place made vivid within the space of a sentence . . . [This novel] shows that fiction, at least, is a country where old men can flourish'

Herald

'Even the spare best of Elmore Leonard would have trouble beating this neo-Western in a foot race . . . This is no mere thriller. Like all McCarthy's books, *No Country For Old Men* meditates on the battle between good and evil in men and society . . . McCarthy is smart to keep this vastly readable book short. The novel rockets forward like a bullet train . . . It ensnares us with its smooth surface, then coaxes us into blackness. Normally, after finishing a book like this, we are meant to return to our cosier world with relief. This book's dark spell means that doing so is impossible – at least for a day or two'

Scotland on Sunday

'McCarthy's prose is never less than knowingly and superbly tailored, honed and polished to its very specific and powerful purpose, combining here the simple-seeming language of Jim Thompson with the lyrical and evocative toughness of William Faulkner . . . Since the publication of *Suttree* over 20 years ago, hardly a reviewer here or in the US has considered a new McCarthy novel without recourse to the word "masterpiece". It is easy to understand why. *No Country for Old Men* is a compelling, harrowing, disturbing, sad, endlessly surprising and resonant novel'

Robert Edric, *Spectator*

NO COUNTRY FOR OLD MEN

Cormac McCarthy is the author of eight previous novels, and among his honours are the National Book Award and the National Book Critics Circle Award.

CORMAC McCARTHY

NO COUNTRY FOR OLD MEN

PICADOR

First published 2005 as a Borzoi Book by Alfred A. Knopf,
a division of Random House, Inc., New York, and simultaneously
in Canada by Random House of Canada Limited, Toronto

First published in Great Britain 2005 by Picador

First published in paperback 2005 by Picador

This edition first published 2006 by Picador
an imprint of Pan Macmillan Ltd
Pan Macmillan, 20 New Wharf Road, London N1 9RR
Basingstoke and Oxford
Associated companies throughout the world
www.panmacmillan.com

ISBN-13: 978-0-330-44011-0
ISBN-10: 0-330-44011-X

Copyright © M-71, Ltd. 2005

A portion of this work previously appeared in *The Virginia Quarterly Review*

The right of Cormac McCarthy to be identified as the
author of this work has been asserted by him in accordance
with the Copyright, Designs and Patents Act 1988.

3 5 7 9 8 6 4 2

A CIP catalogue record for this book is available from
the British Library.

Printed and bound in Great Britain by
Mackays of Chatham plc, Chatham, Kent

All Pan Macmillan titles are available from
www.panmacmillan.com
or from Bookpost by telephoning +44 (0)1624 677237

The author would like to express his appreciation to the Santa Fe Institute for his long association and his four-year residence. He would also like to thank Amanda Urban.

NO COUNTRY FOR OLD MEN

I

I sent one boy to the gaschamber at Huntsville. One and only one. My arrest and my testimony. I went up there and visited with him two or three times. Three times. The last time was the day of his execution. I didnt have to go but I did. I sure didnt want to. He'd killed a fourteen year old girl and I can tell you right now I never did have no great desire to visit with him let alone go to his execution but I done it. The papers said it was a crime of passion and he told me there wasnt no passion to it. He'd been datin this girl, young as she was. He was nineteen. And he told me that he had been plannin to kill somebody for about as long as he could remember. Said that if they turned him out he'd do it again. Said he knew he was goin to hell. Told it to me out of his own mouth. I dont know what to make of that. I surely dont. I thought I'd never seen a person like that and it got me to wonderin if maybe he was some new kind. I watched them strap him into the seat and shut the door. He might of looked a bit nervous about it but that was about all. I really believe that he knew he was goin to be in hell in fifteen minutes. I believe that. And I've thought about that a lot. He was not hard to talk to. Called me Sheriff. But I didnt know what to say to him. What do you say to a man that by his own admission has no soul? Why would you say anything? I've thought about it a good deal. But he wasnt nothin compared to what was comin down the pike.

They say the eyes are the windows to the soul. I dont know what them eyes was the windows to and I guess I'd as soon not know. But there is another view of the world out there and other eyes to see it and that's where this is goin. It has done brought me to a place in my life I would not of thought I'd of come to. Somewhere out there is a true and living prophet of destruction and I dont want to confront him. I know he's real. I have seen his work. I walked in front of those eyes once. I wont do it again. I wont push my chips forward and stand up and go out to meet him. It aint just bein older. I wish that it was. I cant say that it's even what you are willin to do. Because I always knew that you had to be willin to die to even do this job. That was always true. Not to sound glorious about it or nothin but you do. If you aint they'll know it. They'll see it in a heartbeat. I think it is more like what you are willin to become. And I think a man would have to put his soul at hazard. And I wont do that. I think now that maybe I never would.

The deputy left Chigurh standing in the corner of the office with his hands cuffed behind him while he sat in the swivelchair and took off his hat and put his feet up and called Lamar on the mobile.

Just walked in the door. Sheriff he had some sort of thing on him like one of them oxygen tanks for emphysema or whatever. Then he had a hose that run down the inside of his sleeve and went to one of them stunguns like they use at the slaughterhouse. Yessir. Well that's what it looks like. You can see it when you get in. Yessir. I got it covered. Yessir.

When he stood up out of the chair he swung the keys off his belt and opened the locked desk drawer to get the keys to the jail. He was slightly bent over when Chigurh squatted and scooted his manacled hands beneath him to the back of his knees. In the same motion he sat and rocked backward and passed the chain under his feet and then stood instantly and effortlessly. If it looked like a thing he'd practiced many times it was. He dropped his cuffed hands over the deputy's head and leaped into the air and slammed both knees against the back of the deputy's neck and hauled back on the chain.

They went to the floor. The deputy was trying to get his

hands inside the chain but he could not. Chigurh lay there pulling back on the bracelets with his knees between his arms and his face averted. The deputy was flailing wildly and he'd begun to walk sideways over the floor in a circle, kicking over the wastebasket, kicking the chair across the room. He kicked shut the door and he wrapped the throwrug in a wad about them. He was gurgling and bleeding from the mouth. He was strangling on his own blood. Chigurh only hauled the harder. The nickelplated cuffs bit to the bone. The deputy's right carotid artery burst and a jet of blood shot across the room and hit the wall and ran down it. The deputy's legs slowed and then stopped. He lay jerking. Then he stopped moving altogether. Chigurh lay breathing quietly, holding him. When he got up he took the keys from the deputy's belt and released himself and put the deputy's revolver in the waistband of his trousers and went into the bathroom.

He ran cold water over his wrists until they stopped bleeding and he tore strips from a handtowel with his teeth and wrapped his wrists and went back into the office. He sat on the desk and fastened the toweling with tape from a dispenser, studying the dead man gaping up from the floor. When he was done he got the deputy's wallet out of his pocket and took the money and put it in the pocket of his shirt and dropped the wallet to the floor. Then he picked up his airtank and the stungun and walked out the door and got into the deputy's car and started the engine and backed around and pulled out and headed up the road.

On the interstate he picked out a late model Ford sedan with a single driver and turned on the lights and hit the siren briefly. The car pulled onto the shoulder. Chigurh pulled in behind him and shut off the engine and slung the tank across his shoulder and stepped out. The man was watching him in the rearview mirror as he walked up.

What's the problem, officer? he said.

Sir would you mind stepping out of the vehicle?

The man opened the door and stepped out. What's this about? he said.

Would you step away from the vehicle please.

The man stepped away from the vehicle. Chigurh could see the doubt come into his eyes at this bloodstained figure before him but it came too late. He placed his hand on the man's head like a faith healer. The pneumatic hiss and click of the plunger sounded like a door closing. The man slid soundlessly to the ground, a round hole in his forehead from which the blood bubbled and ran down into his eyes carrying with it his slowly uncoupling world visible to see. Chigurh wiped his hand with his handkerchief. I just didnt want you to get blood on the car, he said.

Moss sat with the heels of his boots dug into the volcanic gravel of the ridge and glassed the desert below him with a pair of twelve power german binoculars. His hat pushed back on his head. Elbows propped on his knees. The rifle strapped over his shoulder with a harness-leather sling was a heavybarreled .270 on a '98 Mauser action with a laminated stock of maple and walnut. It carried a Unertl telescopic sight of the same power as the binoculars. The antelope were a little under a mile away. The sun was up less than an hour and the shadow of the ridge and the datilla and the rocks fell far out across the floodplain below him. Somewhere out there was the shadow of Moss himself. He lowered the binoculars and sat studying the land. Far to the south the raw mountains of Mexico. The breaks of the river. To the west the baked terracotta terrain of the running borderlands. He spat dryly and wiped his mouth on the shoulder of his cotton workshirt.

The rifle would shoot half minute of angle groups. Five inch groups at one thousand yards. The spot he'd picked to shoot from lay just below a long talus of lava scree and it would put him well within that distance. Except that it would take the better part of an hour to get there and the antelope were grazing away from him. The best he could say about any of it was that there was no wind.

When he got to the foot of the talus he raised himself slowly and looked for the antelope. They'd not moved far from where he last saw them but the shot was still a good seven hundred yards. He studied the animals through the binoculars. In the compressed air motes and heat distortion. A low haze of shimmering dust and pollen. There was no other cover and there wasnt going to be any other shot.

He wallowed down in the scree and pulled off one boot and laid it over the rocks and lowered the forearm of the rifle down into the leather and pushed off the safety with his thumb and sighted through the scope.

They stood with their heads up, all of them, looking at him.

Damn, he whispered. The sun was behind him so they couldnt very well have seen light reflect off the glass of the scope. They had just flat seen him.

The rifle had a Canjar trigger set to nine ounces and he pulled the rifle and the boot toward him with great care and sighted again and jacked the crosshairs slightly up the back of the animal standing most broadly to him. He knew the exact drop of the bullet in hundred yard increments. It was the distance that was uncertain. He laid his finger in the curve of the trigger. The boar's tooth he wore on a gold chain spooled onto the rocks inside his elbow.

Even with the heavy barrel and the muzzlebrake the rifle bucked up off the rest. When he pulled the animals back into the scope he could see them all standing as before. It took the 150 grain bullet the better part of a second to get there but it took the sound twice that. They were standing looking at the plume of dust where the bullet had hit. Then they bolted. Running almost immediately at top speed out upon the barrial with the long whaang of the rifleshot rolling after them and caroming off the rocks and yawing back across the open country in the early morning solitude.

He stood and watched them go. He raised the glasses. One of the animals had dropped back and was packing one leg and he thought that the round had probably skipped off the pan and caught him in the left hindquarters. He leaned and spat. Damn, he said.

He watched them out of sight beyond the rocky headlands to the south. The pale orange dust that hung in the windless morning light grew faint and then it too was gone. The barrial stood silent and empty in the sun. As if nothing had occurred there at all. He sat and pulled on his boot and picked up the rifle and ejected the spent casing and put it in his shirtpocket and closed the bolt. Then he slung the rifle over his shoulder and set out.

It took him some forty minutes to cross the barrial. From there he made his way up a long volcanic slope and followed the crest of the ridge southeast to an overlook above the country into which the animals had vanished. He glassed the terrain slowly. Crossing that ground was a large tailless dog, black in color. He watched it. It had a huge head and cropped ears and it was limping badly. It paused and stood. It looked behind it. Then it went on. He lowered the glasses and stood watching it go.

He hiked on along the ridge with his thumb hooked in the shoulderstrap of the rifle, his hat pushed back on his head. The back of his shirt was already wet with sweat. The rocks there were etched with pictographs perhaps a thousand years old. The men who drew them hunters like himself. Of them there was no other trace.

At the end of the ridge was a rockslide, a rough trail leading down. Candelilla and scrub catclaw. He sat in the rocks and steadied his elbows on his knees and scanned the country with the binoculars. A mile away on the floodplain sat three vehicles.

He lowered the binoculars and looked over the country at large. Then he raised them again. There looked to be men lying on the ground. He jacked his boots into the rocks and adjusted the focus. The vehicles were four wheel drive trucks or Broncos with big all-terrain tires and winches and racks of rooflights. The men appeared to be dead. He lowered the glasses. Then he raised them again. Then he lowered them and just sat there. Nothing moved. He sat there for a long time.

When he approached the trucks he had the rifle unslung and cradled at his waist with the safety off. He stopped. He studied the country and then he studied the trucks. They were all shot up. Some of the tracks of holes that ran across the sheetmetal were spaced and linear and he knew they'd been put there with automatic weapons. Most of the glass was shot out and the tires flat. He stood there. Listening.

In the first vehicle there was a man slumped dead over the wheel. Beyond were two more bodies lying in the gaunt yellow grass. Dried blood black on the ground. He stopped and listened. Nothing. The drone of flies. He walked around the end of the truck. There was a large dead dog there of the kind he'd seen crossing the floodplain. The dog was gutshot. Beyond that was a third body lying face down. He looked through the window at the man in the truck. He was shot through the head. Blood everywhere. He walked on to the second vehicle but it was empty. He walked out to where the third body lay. There was a shotgun in the grass. The shotgun had a short barrel and it was fitted with a pistol stock and a twenty round drum magazine. He nudged the man's boot with his toe and studied the low surrounding hills.

The third vehicle was a Bronco with a lifted suspension and dark smoked windows. He reached up and opened the driver side door. There was a man sitting in the seat looking at him.

Moss stumbled back, leveling the rifle. The man's face was bloody. He moved his lips dryly. Agua, cuate, he said. Agua, por dios.

He had a shortbarreled H&K machinepistol with a black

nylon shoulderstrap lying in his lap and Moss reached and got it and stepped back. Agua, the man said. Por dios.

I aint got no water.

Agua.

Moss left the door open and slung the H&K over his shoulder and stepped away. The man followed him with his eyes. Moss walked around the front of the truck and opened the door on the other side. He lifted the latch and folded the seat forward. The cargo space in the rear was covered with a metallic silver tarp. He pulled it back. A load of bricksized parcels each wrapped in plastic. He kept one eye on the man and got out his knife and cut a slit in one of the parcels. A loose brown powder dribbled out. He wet his forefinger and dipped it in the powder and smelled it. Then he wiped his finger on his jeans and pulled the tarp back over the parcels and stepped back and looked over the country again. Nothing. He walked away from the truck and stood and glassed the low hills. The lava ridge. The flat country to the south. He got out his handkerchief and walked back and wiped clean everything he'd touched. The doorhandle and the seatlatch and the tarp and the plastic package. He crossed around to the other side of the truck and wiped everything down there too. He tried to think what else he might have touched. He went back to the first truck and opened the door with his kerchief and looked in. He opened the glovebox and closed it again. He studied the dead man at the wheel. He left the door open and walked around to the driver side. The door was full of bulletholes. The windshield. Small caliber. Six millimeter. Maybe number four buckshot. The pattern of them. He opened the door and pushed the windowbutton but the ignition was not on. He shut the door and stood there, studying the low hills.

He squatted and unslung the rifle from off his shoulder and laid it in the grass and took the H&K and pushed back the follower with the heel of his hand. There was a live round in the chamber but the magazine held only two more rounds. He sniffed at the muzzle of the piece. He ejected the clip and slung the rifle over one shoulder and the machinepistol over the other and walked back to the Bronco and held the clip up for the man to see. Otra, he said. Otra.

The man nodded. En mi bolsa.

You speak english?

He didnt answer. He was trying to gesture with his chin. Moss could see two clips sticking out of the canvas pocket of the jacket he was wearing. He reached into the cab and got them and stepped back. Smell of blood and fecal matter. He put one of the full clips into the machinepistol and the other two in his pocket. Agua, cuate, the man said.

Moss scanned the surrounding country. I told you, he said. I aint got no water.

La puerta, the man said.

Moss looked at him.

La puerta. Hay lobos.

There aint no lobos.

Sí, sí. Lobos. Leones.

Moss shut the door with his elbow.

He went back to the first truck and stood looking at the open door on the passenger side. There were no bulletholes in the door but there was blood on the seat. The key was still in the ignition and he reached in and turned it and then pushed the windowbutton. The glass ratcheted slowly up out of the channel. There were two bulletholes in it and a fine spray of dried blood on the inside of the glass. He stood there thinking about that. He looked at the ground. Stains of blood in the clay. Blood in the grass. He looked out down the track south across the caldera back the way the truck had come. There had to be a last man standing. And it wasnt the cuate in the Bronco begging for water.

He walked out on the floodplain and cut a wide circle to see where the track of the tires in the thin grass would show in the sun. He cut for sign a hundred feet to the south. He picked up the man's trail and followed it until he came to blood in the grass. Then more blood.

You aint goin far, he said. You may think you are. But you aint.

He quit the track altogether and walked out to the highest ground visible holding the H&K under his arm with the safety off. He glassed the country to the south. Nothing. He stood fingering the boar's tusk at the front of his shirt. About now, he said, you're shaded up somewheres watchin your backtrack. And the chances of me seein you fore you see me are about as close to nothin as you can get without fallin in.

He squatted and steadied his elbows on his knees and with the binoculars swept the rocks at the head of the valley. He sat and crossed his legs and went over the terrain more slowly and then lowered the glasses and just sat. Do not, he said, get your dumb ass shot out here. Do not do that.

He turned and looked at the sun. It was about eleven oclock. We dont even know that all of this went down last night. It could of been two nights ago. It might even could of been three.

Or it could of been last night.

A light wind had come up. He pushed back his hat and wiped his forehead with his bandanna and put the bandanna back in the hip pocket of his jeans. He looked across the caldera toward the low range of rock on the eastern perimeter.

Nothin wounded goes uphill, he said. It just dont happen.

It was a good hard climb to the top of the ridge and it was close to noon by the time he got there. Far off to the north he could see the shape of a tractor-trailer moving across the shimmering landscape. Ten miles. Maybe fifteen. Highway 90. He sat and swept the new country with the glasses. Then he stopped.

At the foot of a rockslide on the edge of the bajada was a small piece of something blue. He watched it for a long time through the binoculars. Nothing moved. He studied the country about. Then he watched it some more. It was the better part of an hour before he rose and started down.

The dead man was lying against a rock with a nickelplated government .45 automatic lying cocked in the grass between his legs. He'd been sitting up and had slid over sideways. His eyes were open. He looked like he was studying something small in the grass. There was blood on the ground and blood on the rock behind him. The blood was still a dark red but then it was still shaded from the sun. Moss picked up the pistol and pressed the grip safety with his thumb and lowered the hammer. He squatted and tried to wipe the blood off the grips on the leg of the man's trousers but the blood was too well congealed. He stood and stuck the gun in his belt at the small of his back and pushed back his hat and blotted the sweat from his forehead with his shirtsleeve. He turned and stood studying the countryside. There was a heavy leather document case standing upright alongside the dead man's knee and Moss absolutely knew what was in the case and he was scared in a way that he didnt even understand.

When he finally picked it up he just walked out a little ways and sat down in the grass and slid the rifle off his shoulder and laid it aside. He sat with his legs spaced and the H&K in his lap and the case standing between his knees. Then he reached and unbuckled the two straps and unsnapped the brass latch and lifted the flap and folded it back.

It was level full of hundred dollar banknotes. They were

in packets fastened with banktape stamped each with the denomination $10,000. He didnt know what it added up to but he had a pretty good idea. He sat there looking at it and then he closed the flap and sat with his head down. His whole life was sitting there in front of him. Day after day from dawn till dark until he was dead. All of it cooked down into forty pounds of paper in a satchel.

He raised his head and looked out across the bajada. A light wind from the north. Cool. Sunny. One oclock in the afternoon. He looked at the man lying dead in the grass. His good crocodile boots that were filled with blood and turning black. The end of his life. Here in this place. The distant mountains to the south. The wind in the grass. The quiet. He latched the case and fastened the straps and buckled them and rose and shouldered the rifle and then picked up the case and the machinepistol and took his bearings by his shadow and set out.

He thought he knew how to get to his truck and he also thought about wandering through the desert in the dark. There were Mojave rattlesnakes in that country and if he got bit out here at night he would in all likelihood be joining the other members of the party and the document case and its contents would then pass on to some other owner. Weighed against these considerations was the problem of crossing open ground in broad daylight on foot with a fully automatic weapon slung across one shoulder and carrying a satchel containing several million dollars. Beyond all this was the dead certainty that someone was going to come looking for the money. Maybe several someones.

He thought about going back and getting the shotgun with the drum magazine. He was a strong believer in the shotgun. He even thought about leaving the machinepistol behind. It was a penitentiary offense to own one.

He didnt leave anything behind and he didnt go back to the trucks. He set out across country, cutting through the gaps in the volcanic ridges and crossing the flat or rolling country between. Until late in the day he reached the ranch road he'd come down that morning in the dark so long ago. Then in about a mile he came to the truck.

He opened the door and stood the rifle in the floor. He went around and opened the driver door and pushed the lever and slid the seat forward and set the case and the machinepistol behind it. He laid the .45 and the binoculars in the seat and climbed in and pushed the seat back as far as it would go and put the key in the ignition. Then he took off his hat and leaned back and just rested his head against the cold glass behind him and closed his eyes.

When he got to the highway he slowed and rattled over the bars of the cattleguard and then pulled out onto the blacktop and turned on the headlights. He drove west toward Sanderson and he kept to the speed limit every mile of the way. He stopped at the gas station on the east end of town for cigarettes and a long drink of water and then drove on to the Desert Aire and pulled up in front of the trailer and shut off the motor. The lights were on inside. You live to be a hundred, he said, and there wont be another day like this one. As soon as he said it he was sorry.

He got his flashlight from the glovebox and climbed out and took the machinepistol and the case from behind the seat and crawled up under the trailer. He lay there in the dirt looking up at the underside of it. Cheap plastic pipe and plywood. Bits of insulation. He wedged the H&K up into a corner and pulled the insulation down over it and lay there thinking. Then he crawled back out with the case and dusted himself off and climbed the steps and went in.

She was sprawled across the sofa watching TV and drinking a Coke. She didnt even look up. Three oclock, she said.

I can come back later.

She looked at him over the back of the sofa and looked at the television again. What have you got in that satchel?

It's full of money.

Yeah. That'll be the day.

He went into the kitchen and got a beer out of the refrigerator.

Can I have the keys? she said.

Where you goin.

Get some cigarettes.

Cigarettes.

Yes, Llewelyn. Cigarettes. I been settin here all day.

What about cyanide? How are we fixed for that?

Just let me have the keys. I'll set out in the damn yard and smoke.

He took a sip of the beer and went on back into the bedroom and dropped to one knee and shoved the case under the bed. Then he came back. I got you some cigarettes, he said. Let me get em.

He left the beer on the counter and went out and got the two packs of cigarettes and the binoculars and the pistol and slung the .270 over his shoulder and shut the truck door and came back in. He handed her the cigarettes and went on back to the bedroom.

Where'd you get that pistol? she called.

At the gettin place.

Did you buy that thing?

No. I found it.

She sat up on the sofa. Llewelyn?

He came back in. What? he said. Quit hollerin.

What did you give for that thing?

You dont need to know everthing.

How much.

I told you. I found it.

No you never done no such a thing.

He sat on the sofa and put his legs up on the coffeetable and sipped the beer. It dont belong to me, he said. I didnt buy no pistol.

You better not of.

She opened one of the packs of cigarettes and took one out and lit it with a lighter. Where have you been all day?

Went to get you some cigarettes.

I dont even want to know. I dont even want to know what all you been up to.

He sipped the beer and nodded. That'll work, he said.

I think it's better just to not even know even.

You keep runnin that mouth and I'm goin to take you back there and screw you.

Big talk.

Just keep it up.

That's what she said.

Just let me finish this beer. We'll see what she said and what she didnt say.

When he woke it was 1:06 by the digital clock on the bedside table. He lay there looking at the ceiling, the raw glare of the vaporlamp outside bathing the bedroom in a cold and bluish light. Like a winter moon. Or some other kind of moon. Something stellar and alien in its light that he'd come to feel comfortable with. Anything but sleep in the dark.

He swung his feet from under the covers and sat up. He looked at her naked back. Her hair on the pillow. He reached and pulled the blanket up over her shoulder and got up and went into the kitchen.

He took the jar of water from the refrigerator and unscrewed the cap and stood there drinking in the light of the open refrigerator door. Then he just stood there holding the jar with the water beading cold on the glass, looking out the window and down the highway toward the lights. He stood there for a long time.

When he went back to the bedroom he got his shorts off the floor and put them on and went into the bathroom and shut the door. Then he went through into the second bedroom and pulled the case from under the bed and opened it.

He sat in the floor with the case between his legs and delved down into the bills and dredged them up. The packets were twenty deep. He shoved them back down into the case and jostled the case on the floor to level the money. Times twelve. He could do the math in his head. Two point four million. All used bills. He sat looking at it. You have to take this seriously, he said. You cant treat it like luck.

He closed the bag and redid the fasteners and shoved it under the bed and rose and stood looking out the window at the stars over the rocky escarpment to the north of the town. Dead quiet. Not even a dog. But it wasnt the money that he woke up about. Are you dead out there? he said. Hell no, you aint dead.

She woke while he was getting dressed and turned in the bed to watch him.

Llewelyn?

Yeah.

What are you doin?

Gettin dressed.

Where are you goin?

Out.

Where are you goin, baby?

Somethin I forgot to do. I'll be back.

What are you goin to do?

He opened the drawer and took the .45 out and ejected the clip and checked it and put it back and put the pistol in his belt. He turned and looked at her.

I'm fixin to go do somethin dumbern hell but I'm goin anyways. If I dont come back tell Mother I love her.

Your mother's dead Llewelyn.

Well I'll tell her myself then.

She sat up in the bed. You're scarin the hell out of me, Llewelyn. Are you in some kind of trouble?

No. Go to sleep.

Go to sleep?

I'll be back in a bit.

Damn you, Llewelyn.

He stepped back into the doorway and looked at her. What if I was to not come back? Is them your last words?

She followed him down the hallway to the kitchen pulling on her robe. He took an empty gallon jug from under the sink and stood filling it at the tap.

Do you know what time it is? she said.

Yeah. I know what time it is.

Baby I dont want you to go. Where are you goin? I dont want you to go.

Well darlin we're eye to eye on that cause I dont want to go neither. I'll be back. Dont wait up on me.

He pulled in at the filling station under the lights and shut off the motor and got the survey map from the glovebox and unfolded it across the seat and sat there studying it. He finally marked where he thought the trucks should be and then he traced a route cross country back to Harkle's cattle-gate. He had a good set of all-terrain tires on the truck and two spares in the bed but this was some hard country. He sat looking at the line he'd drawn. Then he bent and studied the terrain and drew another one. Then he just sat there looking at the map. When he started the engine and pulled out onto the highway it was two-fifteen in the morning, the road deserted, the truck radio in this outland country dead even of static from one end of the band to the other.

He parked at the gate and got out and opened it and drove through and got out and closed it again and stood listening to the silence. Then he got back in the truck and drove south on the ranch road.

He kept the truck in two wheel drive and drove in second gear. The light of the unrisen moon before him spread out along the dark placard hills like scrimlights in a theatre. Turning below where he'd parked that morning onto what may have been an old wagonroad that bore eastward across

Harkle's land. When the moon did rise it sat swollen and pale and ill formed among the hills to light up all the land about and he turned off the headlights of the truck.

A half hour on he parked and walked out along the crest of a rise and stood looking over the country to the east and to the south. The moon up. A blue world. Visible shadows of clouds crossing the floodplain. Hurrying on the slopes. He sat in the scabrock with his boots crossed before him. No coyotes. Nothing. For a Mexican dopedealer. Yeah. Well. Everbody is somethin.

When he got back to the truck he left the trace and steered by the moon. He crossed under a volcanic headland at the upper end of the valley and turned south again. He had a good memory for country. He was crossing terrain he'd scouted from the ridge earlier that day and he stopped again and got out to listen. When he came back to the truck he pried the plastic cover from the domelight and took the bulb out and put it in the ashtray. He sat with the flashlight and studied the map again. When next he stopped he just shut off the engine and sat with the window down. He sat there for a long time.

He parked the truck a half mile above the upper end of the caldera and got the plastic jug of water out of the floor and put the flashlight in his hip pocket. Then he took the .45 off the seat and shut the door quietly with his thumb on the latchbutton and turned and set off toward the trucks.

They were as he'd left them, hunkered down on their shot-out tires. He approached with the .45 cocked in his hand. Dead quiet. Could be because of the moon. His own shadow was more company than he would have liked. Ugly feeling out here. A trespasser. Among the dead. Dont get weird on me, he said. You aint one of em. Not yet.

The door of the Bronco was open. When he saw that he dropped to one knee. He set the waterjug on the ground. You dumb-ass, he said. Here you are. Too dumb to live.

He turned slowly, skylighting the country. The only thing he could hear was his heart. He made his way to the truck and crouched by the open door. The man had fallen sideways over the console. Still trussed in the shoulderbelt. Fresh blood everywhere. Moss took the flashlight from his pocket and shrouded the lens in his fist and turned it on. He'd been shot through the head. No lobos. No leones. He shone the hooded light into the cargo space behind the seats. Everything gone. He switched off the light and stood. He walked out slowly to where the other bodies lay. The shotgun was gone. The moon was already a quarter ways up. All but day bright. He felt like something in a jar.

He was half way back up the caldera to his truck when something made him stop. He crouched, holding the cocked pistol across his knee. He could see the truck in the moonlight at the top of the rise. He looked off to one side of it to see it the better. There was someone standing beside it. Then they were gone. There is no description of a fool, he said, that you fail to satisfy. Now you're goin to die.

He shoved the .45 into the back of his belt and set off at a trot for the lava ridge. In the distance he heard a truck start. Lights came on at the top of the rise. He began to run.

By the time he got to the rocks the truck was half way down the caldera, the lights bobbing over the bad ground. He looked for something to hide behind. No time. He lay face down with his head between his forearms in the grass and waited. Either they'd seen him or they hadnt. He waited. The truck went by. When it was gone he rose and began to clamber up the slope.

Half way up he stopped and stood sucking air and trying to listen. The lights were somewhere below him. He couldnt see them. He climbed on. After a while he could see the dark shapes of the vehicles down there. Then the truck came back up the caldera with the lights off.

He lay flattened against the rocks. A spotlight went skittering over the lava and back again. The truck slowed. He could hear the engine idling. The slow lope of the cam. Big block engine. The spotlight swept over the rocks again. It's all right, he said. You need to be put out of your misery. Be the best thing for everbody.

The engine revved slightly and idled down again. Deep guttural tone to the exhaust. Cam and headers and God knows what else. After a while it moved on in the dark.

When he got to the crest of the ridge he crouched and took the .45 out of his belt and uncocked it and put it back again and looked out to the north and to the east. No sign of the truck.

How would you like to be out there in your old pickup tryin to outrun that thing? he said. Then he realized that he would never see his truck again. Well, he said. There's lots of things you aint goin to see again.

The spotlight came on again at the head of the caldera and moved across the ridge. Moss lay on his stomach watching. It came back again.

If you knew there was somebody out here afoot that had two million dollars of your money, at what point would you quit lookin for em?

That's right. There aint no such a point.

He lay listening. He couldnt hear the truck. After a while he rose and made his way down the far side of the ridge. Studying the country. The floodplain out there broad and quiet in the moonlight. No way to cross it and nowhere else to go. Well Bubba, what are your plans now?

It's four oclock in the mornin. Do you know where your darlin boy is at?

I'll tell you what. Why dont you just get in your truck and go on out there and take the son of a bitch a drink of water?

The moon was high and small. He kept his eye on the plain below as he climbed along the slope. How motivated are you? he said.

Pretty damn motivated.

You better be.

He could hear the truck. It came around the foreland head of the ridge with the lights off and started down the edge of the floodplain in the moonlight. He flattened himself in the rocks. In addition to the other bad news his thoughts ran to scorpions and rattlesnakes. The spotlight kept rowing back and forth across the face of the ridge. Methodically. Bright shuttle, dark loom. He didnt move.

The truck crossed to the other side and came back. Tooling along in second gear, stopping, the motor loping. He pushed himself forward to where he could see it better. Blood kept running into his eye from a cut in his forehead. He didnt even know where he'd gotten it. He wiped his eye with the heel of his hand and wiped his hand on his jeans. He took out his kerchief and pressed it to his head.

You could head south to the river.

Yeah. You could.

Less open ground.

Less aint none.

He turned, still holding the handkerchief to his forehead. No cloud cover in sight.

You need to be somewhere come daylight.

Home in bed would be good.

He studied the blue floodplain out there in the silence. A vast and breathless amphitheatre. Waiting. He'd had this feeling before. In another country. He never thought he'd have it again.

He waited a long time. The truck didnt come back. He made his way south along the ridge. He stood and listened. Not a coyote, nothing.

By the time he'd descended onto the river plain the sky to the east carried the first faint wash of light. It was the darkest this night was going to get. The plain ran to the breaks of the river and he listened one last time and then set out at a trot.

It was a long trek and he was still some two hundred yards from the river when he heard the truck. A raw gray light was breaking over the hills. When he looked back he could see the dust against the new skyline. Still the better part of a mile away. In the dawn quiet the sound of it no more sinister than a boat on a lake. Then he heard it downshift. He pulled the .45 from his belt so that he wouldnt lose it and set out at a dead run.

When he looked back again it had closed a good part of the distance. He was still a hundred yards from the river and he didnt know what he'd find when he got there. A sheer rock gorge. The first long panes of light were standing through a gap in the mountains to the east and fanning over the country before him. The truck was ablaze with lights, roof rack and bumper spots. The engine kept racing away into a howl where the wheels left the ground.

They wont shoot you, he said. They cant afford to do that.

The long crack of a rifle went caroming out over the pan. What he'd heard whisper overhead he realized was the round passing and vanishing toward the river. He looked back and there was a man standing up out of the sunroof, one hand on top of the cab, the other cradling a rifle upright.

Where he reached the river it made a broad sweep out of a canyon and carried down past great stands of carrizo cane. Downriver it washed up against a rock bluff and then bore away to the south. Darkness deep in the canyon. The water dark. He dropped into the cut and fell and rolled and rose and began to make his way down a long sandy ridge toward the river. He hadnt gone twenty feet before he realized that he had no time to do that. He glanced back once at the rim and then squatted and shoved himself off down the side of the slope, holding the .45 before him in both hands.

He rolled and slid a good ways, his eyes almost shut against the dust and sand he was plowing up, the pistol clutched to his chest. Then all that stopped and he was simply falling. He opened his eyes. The fresh world of morning above him, turning slowly.

He slammed into a gravel bank and gave out a groan. Then he was rolling through some sort of rough grass. He came to a stop and lay there on his stomach gasping for air.

The pistol was gone. He crawled back through the flattened grass until he found it and he picked it up and turned to scan the rim of the river breaks above him, whacking the pistolbarrel across his forearm to shake out the dirt. His mouth was full of sand. His eyes. He saw two men appear against the sky and he cocked the pistol and fired at them and they went away again.

He knew he didnt have time to crawl to the river and he just rose and made a run for it, splashing across the braided gravel flats and down a long sandbar until he came to the main channel. He got out his keys and his billfold and buttoned them into his shirtpocket. The cold wind blowing off the water smelled of iron. He could taste it. He threw away the flashlight and lowered the hammer on the .45 and shoved it into the crotch of his jeans. Then he shucked off his boots and pulled them inside his belt upside down at either side and tightened the belt as far as he could pull it and turned and dove into the river.

The cold took his breath. He turned and looked back toward the rim, blowing and backpedaling through the slate-blue water. Nothing there. He turned and swam.

The current carried him down into the bend of the river and hard up against the rocks. He pushed himself off. The bluff above him rose dark and deeply cupped and the water in the shadows was black and choppy. When he finally spilled out into the tailwater and looked back he could see the truck parked at the top of the bluff but he couldnt see anyone. He checked to see that he still had his boots and the gun and then turned and began to stroke for the far shore.

By the time he dragged himself shivering out of the river he was the better part of a mile from where he'd gone in. His socks were gone and he set out at a jog barefoot toward the standing cane. Round cups in the shelving rock where the ancients had ground their meal. When he looked back again the truck was gone. Two men were trotting along the high bluff silhouetted against the sky. He was almost to the cane when it rattled all about him and there was a heavy whump and then the echo of it from across the river.

He was hit in the upper arm by a buckshot and it stung like a hornet. He put his hand over it and dove into the cane, the lead ball half buried in the back of his arm. His left leg kept wanting to give out beneath him and he was having trouble breathing.

Deep in the brake he dropped to his knees and knelt there sucking air. He undid his belt and let the boots drop into the sand and reached down and got the .45 and laid it to one side and felt the back of his arm. The buckshot was gone. He unbuttoned his shirt and took it off and pulled his arm around to see the wound. It was just the shape of the buckshot, bleeding slightly, pieces of shirtfiber packed into it. The whole back of his arm was already becoming an ugly purple bruise. He wrung the water out of his shirt and put it on again and buttoned it and pulled on the boots and stood and buckled his belt. He picked up the pistol and took the clip out of it and ejected the round from the chamber and then shook the gun and blew through the barrel and reassembled it. He didnt know if it would fire or not but he thought it probably would.

When he came out of the cane on the far side he stopped to look back but the cane was thirty feet high and he couldnt see anything. Downriver was a broad bench of land and a stand of cottonwoods. By the time he got there his feet were already beginning to blister from walking barefoot in the wet boots. His arm was swollen and throbbing but the bleeding seemed to have stopped and he walked out into the sun on a gravel bar and sat there and pulled off the boots and looked at the raw red sores on his heels. As soon as he sat down his leg began to hurt again.

He unsnapped the small leather holster at his belt and got out his knife and then stood up and took off his shirt again. He cut off the sleeves at the elbow and sat and wrapped his feet in them and pulled on the boots. He put the knife back in the holster and fastened it and picked up the pistol and stood and listened. A redwing blackbird. Nothing.

As he turned to go he heard the truck very faintly on the far side of the river. He looked for it but he couldnt see it. He thought that by now probably the two men had crossed the river and were somewhere behind him.

He went on through the trees. The trunks silted up from the high water and the roots tangled among the rocks. He took off his boots again to try to cross the gravel without leaving any tracks and he climbed a long and rocky rincon toward the south rim of the river canyon carrying the boots and the wrappings and the pistol and keeping an eye on the terrain below. The sun was in the canyon and the rocks he'd crossed would dry in minutes. At a bench near the rim he stopped and lay on his belly with his boots in the grass beside him. It was only another ten minutes to the top but he didnt think he had ten minutes. On the far side of the river a hawk set forth from the cliffs whistling thinly. He waited. After a while a man came out of the cane upriver and paused and stood. He was carrying a machinegun. A second man emerged below him. They glanced at one another and then came on.

They passed below him and he watched them out of sight down the river. He wasnt really even thinking about them. He was thinking about his truck. When the courthouse opened at nine oclock Monday morning someone was going to be calling in the vehicle number and getting his name and address. This was some twenty-four hours away. By then they would know who he was and they would never stop looking for him. Never, as in never.

He had a brother in California he was supposed to tell what? Arthur there's some old boys on their way down there to see you who propose to lower your balls between the jaws of a six-inch machinist's vise and commence crankin on the handle a quarter turn at a time whether you know where I'm at or not. You might want to think about movin to China.

He sat up and wrapped his feet and pulled the boots on and stood and started up the last stretch of canyon to the rim. Where he crested out the country lay dead flat, stretching away to the south and to the east. Red dirt and creosote. Mountains in the far and middle distance. Nothing out there.

Heatshimmer. He stuck the pistol in his belt and looked down at the river one more time and then set out east. Langtry Texas was thirty miles as the crow flies. Maybe less. Ten hours. Twelve. His feet were already hurting. His leg hurt. His chest. His arm. The river dropped away behind him. He hadnt even taken a drink.

II

I dont know if law enforcement work is more dangerous now than what it used to be or not. I know when I first took office you'd have a fistfight somewheres and you'd go to break it up and they'd offer to fight you. And sometimes you had to accommodate em. They wouldnt have it no other way. And you'd better not lose, neither. You dont see that so much no more, but maybe you see worse. I had a man pull a gun on me one time and it happened that I grabbed it just as he went to fire and the plunger on the hammer went right through the fleshy part of my thumb. You can see the mark of it there. But that man had ever intention of killin me. A few years ago and it wasnt that many neither I was goin out one of these little two lane blacktop roads of a night and I come up on a pickup truck that they was two old boys settin in the bed of it. They kindly blinked in the lights and I backed off some but the truck had Coahuila plates on it and I thought, well, I need to stop these old boys and take a look. So I hit the lights and whenever I done that I seen the slider window in the back of the cab open and here come somebody passin a shotgun out the window to the old boy settin in the bed of the truck. I'll tell you right now I hit them brakes with both feet. It skidded the unit sideways to where the lights was goin out into the brush but the last thing I seen in the bed of the truck was the old boy puttin that shotgun to his shoulder. I hit the seat and I just had hit it when here come the windshield all over me in them little bitty pieces they break up into. I still had one foot on the brake and I could feel the cruiser slidin down into the bar ditch and I thought it was goin to roll but it didnt. It filled the car just full of dirt. The old boy he opened up on me twice more and shot all the glass out of one side of the cruiser and by then I'd come to a stop and I laid there in the seat, had my pistol out, and I heard that pickup leave out and I raised up and fired several shots at the taillights but they was long gone.

Point bein you dont know what all you're stoppin when you do stop somebody. You take out on the highway. You walk up to a car and you dont know what you're liable to find. I set there in that cruiser for a long time. The motor had died but the lights was still on. Cab full of glass and dirt. I got out and kindly shook myself off and got back in and just set there. Just kindly collectin my thoughts. Windshield wipers hangin in on the dashboard. I turned off the lights and I just set there. You take somebody that will actually throw down on a law enforcement officer and open fire, you have got some very serious people. I never saw that truck again. Nobody else did neither. Or not them plates noways. Maybe I should of took out after it. Or tried to. I dont know. I drove back to Sanderson and pulled in at the cafe and I'll tell you they come from all over to see that cruiser. It was shot just full of holes.

Looked like the Bonnie and Clyde car. I didnt have a mark on me. Not even from all that glass. I was criticized for that too. Parkin there like I done. They said I was showin out. Well, maybe I was. But I needed that cup of coffee too, I'll tell you.

I read the papers ever mornin. Mostly I suppose just to try and figure out what might be headed this way. Not that I've done all that good a job at headin it off. It keeps gettin harder. Here a while back they was two boys run into one another and one of em was from California and one from Florida. And they met somewheres or other in between. And then they set out together travelin around the country killin people. I forget how many they did kill. Now what are the chances of a thing like that? Them two had never laid eyes on one another. There cant be that many of em. I dont think. Well, we dont know. Here the other day they was a woman put her baby in a trash compactor. Who would think of such a thing? My wife wont read the papers no more. She's probably right. She generally is.

Bell climbed the rear steps of the courthouse and went down the hall to his office. He swiveled his chair around and sat and looked at the telephone. Go ahead, he said. I'm here.

The phone rang. He reached and picked it up. Sheriff Bell, he said.

He listened. He nodded.

Mrs Downie I believe he'll come down directly. Why dont you call me back here in a little bit. Yes mam.

He took off his hat and put it on the desk and sat with his eyes closed, pinching the bridge of his nose. Yes mam, he said. Yes mam.

Mrs Downie I havent seen that many dead cats in trees. I think he'll come down directly if you'll just leave him be. You call me back in a little bit, you hear?

He hung the phone up and sat looking at it. It's money, he said. You have enough money you dont have to talk to people about cats in trees.

Well. Maybe you do.

The radio squawked. He picked up the receiver and

pushed the button and put his feet up on the desk. Bell, he said.

He sat listening. He lowered his feet to the floor and sat up.

Get the keys and look in the turtle. That's all right. I'm right here.

He drummed his fingers on the desk.

All right. Keep your lights on. I'll be there in fifty minutes. And Torbert? Shut the trunk.

He and Wendell pulled onto the paved shoulder in front of the unit and parked and got out. Torbert got out and was standing by the door of his car. The sheriff nodded. He walked along the edge of the roadway studying the tire tracks. You seen this, I reckon, he said.

Yessir.

Well let's take a look.

Torbert opened the trunk and they stood looking at the body. The front of the man's shirt was covered with blood, partly dried. His whole face was bloody. Bell leaned and reached into the trunk and took something from the man's shirtpocket and unfolded it. It was a bloodstained receipt for gas from a service station in Junction Texas. Well, he said. This was the end of the road for Bill Wyrick.

I didnt look to see if he had a billfold on him.

That's all right. He dont. This here was just dumb luck.

He studied the hole in the man's forehead. Looks like a .45. Clean. Almost like a wadcutter.

What's a wadcutter?

It's a target round. You got the keys?

Yessir.

Bell shut the trunklid. He looked around. Passing trucks on the interstate were downshifting as they approached. I've already talked to Lamar. Told him he can have his unit back in about three days. I called Austin and they're lookin for you first thing in the mornin. I aint loadin him into one of our units and he damn sure dont need a helicopter. You take Lamar's unit back to Sonora when you get done and call and me or Wendell one will come and get you. You got any money?

Yessir.

Fill out the report same as any report.

Yessir.

White male, late thirties, medium build.

How do you spell Wyrick?

You dont spell it. We dont know what his name is.

Yessir.

He might have a family someplace.

Yessir. Sheriff?

Yes.

What do we have on the perpetrator?

We dont. Give Wendell your keys fore you forget it.

They're in the unit.

Well let's not be leavin keys in the units.

Yessir.

I'll see you in two days' time.

Yessir.

I hope that son of a bitch is in California.

Yessir. I know what you mean.

I got a feelin he aint.

Yessir. I do too.

Wendell, you ready?

Wendell leaned and spat. Yessir, he said. I'm ready. He looked at Torbert. You get stopped with that old boy in the turtle just tell em you dont know nothin about it. Tell em somebody must of put him in there while you was havin coffee.

Torbert nodded. You and the sheriff goin to come down and get me off of death row?

If we cant get you out we'll get in there with you.

You all dont be makin light of the dead thataway, Bell said.

Wendell nodded. Yessir, he said. You're right. I might be one myself some day.

Driving out 90 toward the turnoff at Dryden he came across a hawk dead in the road. He saw the feathers move in the wind. He pulled over and got out and walked back and squatted on his bootheels and looked at it. He raised one wing and let it fall again. Cold yellow eye dead to the blue vault above them.

It was a big redtail. He picked it up by one wingtip and carried it to the bar ditch and laid it in the grass. They would hunt the blacktop, sitting on the high powerpoles and watching the highway in both directions for miles. Any small thing that might venture to cross. Closing on their prey against the sun. Shadowless. Lost in the concentration of the hunter. He wouldnt have the trucks running over it.

He stood there looking out across the desert. So quiet. Low hum of wind in the wires. High bloodweeds along the road. Wiregrass and sacahuista. Beyond in the stone arroyos the tracks of dragons. The raw rock mountains shadowed in the late sun and to the east the shimmering abscissa of the desert plains under a sky where raincurtains hung dark as soot all along the quadrant. That god lives in silence who has scoured the following land with salt and ash. He walked back to the cruiser and got in and pulled away.

When he pulled up in front of the sheriff's office in Sonora the first thing he saw was the yellow tape stretched across the parking lot. A small courthouse crowd. He got out and crossed the street.

What's happened, Sheriff?

I dont know, said Bell. I just got here.

He ducked under the tape and went up the steps. Lamar looked up when he tapped at the door. Come in, Ed Tom, he said. Come in. We got hell to pay here.

They walked out on the courthouse lawn. Some of the men followed them.

You all go on, said Lamar. Me and the sheriff here need to talk.

He looked haggard. He looked at Bell and he looked at the ground. He shook his head and looked away. I used to play mumbledypeg here when I was a boy. Right here. These youngsters today I dont think would even know what that was. Ed Tom this is a damned lunatic.

I hear you.

You got anything to go on?

Not really.

Lamar looked away. He wiped his eyes with the back of his sleeve. I'll tell you right now. This son of a bitch will never see a day in court. Not if I catch him he wont.

Well, we need to catch him first.

That boy was married.

I didnt know that.

Twenty-three year old. Clean cut boy. Straight as a die. Now I got to go out to his house fore his wife hears it on the damn radio.

I dont envy you that. I surely dont.

I think I'm goin to quit, Ed Tom.

You want me to go out there with you?

No. I appreciate it. I need to go.

All right.

I just have this feelin we're looking at somethin we really aint never even seen before.

I got the same feelin. Let me call you this evenin.

I appreciate it.

He watched Lamar cross the lawn and climb the steps to his office. I hope you dont quit, he said. I think we're goin to need all of you we can get.

When they pulled up in front of the cafe it was one-twenty in the morning. There were only three people on the bus.

Sanderson, the driver said.

Moss made his way forward. He'd seen the driver eyeing him in the mirror. Listen, he said. Do you think you could let me out down at the Desert Aire? I got a bad leg and I live down there but I got nobody to pick me up.

The driver shut the door. Yeah, he said. I can do that.

When he walked in she got up off the couch and ran and put her arms around his neck. I thought you was dead, she said.

Well I aint so dont go to slobberin.

I aint.

Why dont you fix me some bacon and eggs while I take a shower.

Let me see that cut on your head. What happened to you? Where's your truck at?

I need to take a shower. Fix me somethin to eat. My stomach thinks my throat's been cut.

When he came out of the shower he was wearing a pair of

shorts and when he sat at the little formica table in the kitchen the first thing she said was What's that on the back of your arm?

How many eggs is this?

Four.

You got any more toast?

They's two more pieces comin. What is that, Llewelyn?

What would you like to hear?

The truth.

He sipped his coffee and set about salting his eggs.

You aint goin to tell me, are you?

No.

What happened to your leg?

It's broke out in a rash.

She buttered the fresh toast and put it on the plate and sat in the chair opposite. I like to eat breakfast of a night, he said. Takes me back to my bachelor days.

What is goin on, Llewelyn?

Here's what's goin on, Carla Jean. You need to get your stuff packed and be ready to roll out of here come daylight. Whatever you leave you aint goin to see it again so if you want it dont leave it. There's a bus leaves out of here at seven-fifteen in the mornin. I want you to go to Odessa and wait there till I can call you.

She sat back in the chair and watched him. You want me to go to Odessa, she said.

That's correct.

You aint kiddin, are you?

Me? No. I aint kiddin a bit. Are we out of preserves?

She got up and got the preserves out of the refrigerator and set them on the table and sat back down. He unscrewed the jar and ladled some onto his toast and spread it with his knife.

What's in that satchel you brought in?

I told you what was in that satchel.

You said it was full of money.

Well then I reckon that's what's in it.

Where's it at?

Under the bed in the back room.

Under the bed.

Yes mam.

Can I go back there and look?

You're free white and twenty-one so I reckon you can do whatever you want.

I aint twenty-one.

Well whatever you are.

And you want me to get on a bus and go to Odessa.

You are gettin on a bus and goin to Odessa.

What am I supposed to tell Mama?

Well, try standin in the door and hollerin: Mama, I'm home.

Where's your truck at?

Gone the way of all flesh. Nothin's forever.

How are we supposed to get down there in the mornin?

Call Miss Rosa over yonder. She aint got nothin to do.

What have you done, Llewelyn?

I robbed the bank at Fort Stockton.

You're a lyin sack of you know what.

If you aint goin to believe me what'd you ask me for? You need to get on back there and get your stuff together. We got about four hours till daylight.

Let me see that thing on your arm.

You done seen it.

Let me put somethin on it.

Yeah, I think there's some buckshot salve in the cabinet if we aint out. Will you go on and quit aggravatin me? I'm tryin to eat.

Did you get shot?

No. I just said that to get you stirred up. Go on now.

He crossed the Pecos River just north of Sheffield Texas and took route 349 south. When he pulled into the filling station at Sheffield it was almost dark. A long red twilight with doves crossing the highway heading south toward some ranch tanks. He got change from the proprietor and made a phone call and filled the tank and went back in and paid.

You all gettin any rain up your way? the proprietor said.

Which way would that be?

I seen you was from Dallas.

Chigurh picked his change up off the counter. And what business is it of yours where I'm from, friendo?

I didnt mean nothin by it.

You didnt mean nothing by it.

I was just passin the time of day.

I guess that passes for manners in your cracker view of things.

Well sir, I apologized. If you dont want to accept my apology I dont know what else I can do for you.

How much are these?

Sir?

I said how much are these.

Sixty-nine cents.

Chigurh unfolded a dollar onto the counter. The man rang it up and stacked the change before him the way a dealer places chips. Chigurh hadnt taken his eyes from him. The man looked away. He coughed. Chigurh opened the plastic package of cashews with his teeth and doled a third part of them into his palm and stood eating.

Will there be somethin else? the man said.

I dont know. Will there?

Is there somethin wrong?

With what?

With anything.

Is that what you're asking me? Is there something wrong with anything?

The man turned away and put his fist to his mouth and coughed again. He looked at Chigurh and he looked away. He looked out the window at the front of the store. The gas pumps and the car sitting there. Chigurh ate another small handful of the cashews.

Will there be anything else?

You've already asked me that.

Well I need to see about closin.

See about closing.

Yessir.

What time do you close?

Now. We close now.

Now is not a time. What time do you close.

Generally around dark. At dark.

Chigurh stood slowly chewing. You dont know what you're talking about, do you?

Sir?

I said you dont know what you're talking about do you.

I'm talkin about closin. That's what I'm talkin about.

What time do you go to bed.

Sir?

You're a bit deaf, arent you? I said what time do you go to bed.

Well. I'd say around nine-thirty. Somewhere around nine-thirty.

Chigurh poured more cashews into his palm. I could come back then, he said.

We'll be closed then.

That's all right.

Well why would you be comin back? We'll be closed.

You said that.

Well we will.

You live in that house behind the store?

Yes I do.

You've lived here all your life?

The proprietor took a while to answer. This was my wife's father's place, he said. Originally.

You married into it.

We lived in Temple Texas for many years. Raised a family there. In Temple. We come out here about four years ago.

You married into it.

If that's the way you want to put it.

I dont have some way to put it. That's the way it is.

Well I need to close now.

Chigurh poured the last of the cashews into his palm and wadded the little bag and placed it on the counter. He stood oddly erect, chewing.

You seem to have a lot of questions, the proprietor said. For somebody that dont want to say where it is they're from.

What's the most you ever saw lost on a coin toss?

Sir?

I said what's the most you ever saw lost on a coin toss.

Coin toss?

Coin toss.

I dont know. Folks dont generally bet on a coin toss. It's usually more like just to settle somethin.

What's the biggest thing you ever saw settled?

I dont know.

Chigurh took a twenty-five cent piece from his pocket and flipped it spinning into the bluish glare of the fluorescent lights overhead. He caught it and slapped it onto the back of his forearm just above the bloody wrappings. Call it, he said.

Call it?

Yes.

For what?

Just call it.

Well I need to know what it is we're callin here.

How would that change anything?

The man looked at Chigurh's eyes for the first time. Blue as lapis. At once glistening and totally opaque. Like wet stones. You need to call it, Chigurh said. I cant call it for you. It wouldnt be fair. It wouldnt even be right. Just call it.

I didnt put nothin up.

Yes you did. You've been putting it up your whole life. You just didnt know it. You know what the date is on this coin?

No.

It's nineteen fifty-eight. It's been traveling twenty-two years to get here. And now it's here. And I'm here. And I've got my hand over it. And it's either heads or tails. And you have to say. Call it.

I dont know what it is I stand to win.

In the blue light the man's face was beaded thinly with sweat. He licked his upper lip.

You stand to win everything, Chigurh said. Everything.

You aint makin any sense, mister.

Call it.

Heads then.

Chigurh uncovered the coin. He turned his arm slightly for the man to see. Well done, he said.

He picked the coin from his wrist and handed it across.

What do I want with that?

Take it. It's your lucky coin.

I dont need it.

Yes you do. Take it.

The man took the coin. I got to close now, he said.

Dont put it in your pocket.

Sir?

Dont put it in your pocket.

Where do you want me to put it?

Dont put it in your pocket. You wont know which one it is.

All right.

Anything can be an instrument, Chigurh said. Small things. Things you wouldnt even notice. They pass from hand to hand. People dont pay attention. And then one day there's an accounting. And after that nothing is the same. Well, you say. It's just a coin. For instance. Nothing special there. What could that be an instrument of? You see the problem. To separate the act from the thing. As if the parts of some moment in history might be interchangeable with the parts of some other moment. How could that be? Well, it's just a coin. Yes. That's true. Is it?

Chigurh cupped his hand and scooped his change from the counter into his palm and put the change in his pocket and turned and walked out the door. The proprietor watched him go. Watched him get into the car. The car started and pulled off from the gravel apron onto the highway south. The lights never did come on. He laid the coin on the counter and looked at it. He put both hands on the counter and just stood leaning there with his head bowed.

When he got to Dryden it was about eight oclock. He sat at the intersection in front of Condra's Feed Store with the lights off and the motor running. Then he turned the lights on and pulled out on highway 90 headed east.

The white marks at the side of the road when he found them looked like surveyor's marks but there were no numbers, just the chevrons. He marked the mileage on the odometer and drove another mile and slowed and turned off the highway. He shut off the lights and left the motor running and got out and walked down and opened the gate and came back. He drove across the bars of the cattleguard and got out and closed the gate again and stood there listening. Then he got in the car and drove out down the rutted track.

He followed a southrunning fence, the Ford wallowing over the bad ground. The fence was just an old remnant, three wires strung on mesquite posts. In a mile or so he came out on a gravel plain where a Dodge Ramcharger was parked facing toward him. He pulled slowly alongside it and shut down the engine.

The Ramcharger's windows were tinted so dark they looked black. Chigurh opened the door and got out. A man got out on the passenger side of the Dodge and folded the seat forward and climbed into the rear. Chigurh walked around the vehicle and got in and shut the door. Let's go, he said.

Have you talked to him? the driver said.

No.

He dont know what's happened?

No. Let's go.

They rolled out across the desert in the dark.

When do you aim to tell him? the driver said.

When I know what it is that I'm telling him.

When they came to Moss's truck Chigurh leaned forward to study it.

Is that his truck?

That's it. Plates is gone.

Pull up here. Have you got a screwdriver?

Look in the jockeybox there.

Chigurh got out with the screwdriver and walked over to the truck and opened the door. He pried the aluminum inspection plate off of the rivets inside the door and put it in his pocket and came back and got in and put the screwdriver back in the glovebox. Who cut the tires? he said.

It wasnt us.

Chigurh nodded. Let's go, he said.

They parked some distance from the trucks and walked down to look at them. Chigurh stood there a long time. It was cold out on the barrial and he had no jacket but he didnt seem to notice. The other two men stood waiting. He had a flashlight in his hand and he turned it on and walked among the trucks and looked at the bodies. The two men followed at a small distance.

Whose dog? Chigurh said.

We dont know.

He stood looking in at the dead man slumped across the console of the Bronco. He shone the light into the cargo space behind the seats.

Where's the box? he said.

It's in the truck. You want it?

Can you get anything on it?

No.

Nothing?

Not a bleep.

Chigurh studied the dead man. He jostled him with his flashlight.

These are some ripe petunias, one of the men said.

Chigurh didnt answer. He backed out of the truck and stood looking over the bajada in the moonlight. Dead quiet. The man in the Bronco had not been dead three days or anything like it. He pulled the pistol from the waistband of his trousers and turned around to where the two men were standing and shot them once each through the head in rapid succession and put the gun back in his belt. The second man had actually half turned to look at the first as he fell. Chigurh stepped between them and bent and pulled away the shoulder-strap from the second man and swung up the nine millimeter Glock he'd been carrying and walked back out to the vehicle and got in and started it and backed around and drove up out of the caldera and back toward the highway.

III

I dont know that law enforcement benefits all that much from new technology. Tools that comes into our hands comes into theirs too. Not that you can go back. Or that you'd even want to. We used to have them old Motorola two way radios. We've had the high-band now for several years. Some things aint changed. Common sense aint changed. I'll tell my deputies sometimes to just follow the breadcrumbs. I still like the old Colts. .44-40. If that wont stop him you'd better throw the thing down and take off runnin. I like the old Winchester model 97. I like it that it's got a hammer. I dont like havin to hunt the safety on a gun. Of course some things is worse. That cruiser of mine is seven years old. It's got the 454 in it. You cant get that engine no more. I drove one of the new ones. It wouldnt outrun a fatman. I told the man I thought I'd stick with what I had. That aint always a good policy. But it aint always a bad one neither.

This other thing I dont know. People will ask me about it ever so often. I cant say as I would rule it out altogether. It aint somethin I would like to have to see again. To witness. The ones that really ought to be on death row will never make it. I believe that. You remember certain things about a thing *like that. People didnt know what to wear. There was one or two come dressed in black, which I suppose was all right. Some of the men come just in their shirtsleeves and that kindly bothered me. I aint sure I could tell you why.*

Still they seemed to know what to do and that surprised me. Most of em I know had never been to a execution before. When it was over they pulled this curtain around the gaschamber with him in there settin slumped over and people just got up and filed out. Like out of church or somethin. It just seemed peculiar. Well it was peculiar. I'd have to say it was probably the most unusual day I ever spent.

Quite a few people didnt believe in it. Even them that worked on the row. You'd be surprised. Some of em I think had at one time. You see somebody ever day sometimes for years and then one day you walk that man down the hallway and put him to death. Well. That'll take some of the cackle out of just about anybody. I dont care who it is. And of course some of them boys was not very bright. Chaplain Pickett told me about one he ministered to and he ate his last meal and he'd ordered this dessert, ever what it was. And it come time to go and Pickett he asked him didnt he want his dessert and the old boy told him he was savin it for when he come back. I dont know what to say about that. Pickett didnt neither.

I never had to kill nobody and I am very glad of that fact. Some of the old time sheriffs wouldnt even carry a firearm. A lot of folks find that hard to believe but it's a fact. Jim Scarborough never carried one. That's the younger Jim. Gaston

Boykins wouldnt wear one. Up in Comanche County. I always liked to hear about the old timers. Never missed a chance to do so. The old time concern that the sheriffs had for their people is been watered down some. You cant help but feel it. Nigger Hoskins over in Bastrop County knowed everbody's phone number in the whole county by heart.

It's a odd thing when you come to think about it. The opportunities for abuse are just about everwhere. There's no requirements in the Texas State Constitution for bein a sheriff. Not a one. There is no such thing as a county law. You think about a job where you have pretty much the same authority as God and there is no requirements put upon you and you are charged with preservin nonexistent laws and you tell me if that's peculiar or not. Because I say that it is. Does it work? Yes. Ninety percent of the time. It takes very little to govern good people. Very little. And bad people cant be governed at all. Or if they could I never heard of it.

The bus pulled into Fort Stockton at quarter to nine and Moss stood and got his bag down from the overhead rack and picked up the document case out of the seat and stood looking down at her.

Dont get on a airplane with that thing, she said. They'll put you under the jail.

My mama didnt raise no ignorant children.

When are you goin to call me.

I'll call you in a few days.

All right.

You take care.

I got a bad feelin, Llewelyn.

Well, I got a good one. So they ought to balance out.

I hope so.

I cant call you except from a payphone.

I know it. Call me.

I will. Quit worryin about everthing.

Llewelyn?

What.

Nothin.

What is it.

Nothin. I just wanted to say it.

You take care.

Llewelyn?

What.

Dont hurt nobody. You hear?

He stood there with the bag slung across his shoulder. I aint makin no promises, he said. That's how you get hurt.

Bell had raised the first forkful of his supper to his mouth when the phone rang. He lowered it again. She'd started to push her chair back but he wiped his mouth with his napkin and rose. I'll get it, he said.

All right.

How the hell do they know when you're eatin? We never eat this late.

Dont be cussin, she said.

He picked up the phone. Sheriff Bell, he said.

He listened for a while. Then he said: I'm goin to finish my supper. I'll meet you there in about forty minutes. Just leave the lights on on your unit.

He hung up the phone and came back to his chair and sat and picked up the napkin and put it in his lap and picked up his fork. Somebody called in a car afire, he said. Just this side of Lozier Canyon.

What do you make of that?

He shook his head.

He ate. He drank the last of his coffee. Come go with me, he said.

Let me get my coat.

They pulled off the road at the gate and drove over the cattleguard and pulled up behind Wendell's unit. Wendell walked back and Bell rolled down the window.

It's about a half mile down, Wendell said. Just follow me.

I can see it.

Yessir. It was goin real good here about a hour ago. The people that called it in seen it from the road.

They parked a little way off and got out and stood looking at it. You could feel the heat on your face. Bell came around and opened the door and took his wife's hand. She got out and stood with her arms folded in front of her. There was a pickup truck parked a ways down and two men were standing there in the dull red glare. They nodded each in turn and said Sheriff.

We could of brought weeners, she said.

Yeah. Marshmallers.

You wouldnt think a car would burn like that.

No, you wouldnt. Did you all see anything?

No sir. Just the fire.

Didnt pass nobody or nothin?

No sir.

Does that look to you like about a '77 Ford, Wendell?

It could be.

I'd say it is.

Was that what the old boy was drivin?

Yeah. Dallas plates.

It wasnt his day, was it Sheriff.

It surely wasnt.

Why do you reckon they set fire to it?

I dont know.

Wendell turned and spat. Wasnt what the old boy had in mind when he left Dallas I dont reckon, was it?

Bell shook his head. No, he said. I'd guess it was about the farthest thing from his mind.

In the morning when he got to the office the phone was ringing. Torbert wasnt back yet. He finally called at nine-thirty and Bell sent Wendell to get him. Then he sat with his feet on the desk staring at his boots. He sat that way for some time. Then he picked up the mobile and called Wendell.

Where you at?

Just past Sanderson Canyon.

Turn around and come back.

All right. What about Torbert?

Call him and tell him to just set tight. I'll come get him this afternoon.

Yessir.

Go to the house and get the keys to the truck from Loretta and hook up the horsetrailer. Saddle my horse and Loretta's and load and I'll see you out there in about a hour.

Yessir.

He hung up the speaker and got up and went down to check on the jail.

· · ·

They drove through the gate and closed it again and drove down along the fence about a hundred feet and parked. Wendell unlatched the trailer doors and led the horses out. Bell took the reins of his wife's horse. You ride Winston, he said.

You sure?

Oh I'm more than sure. Anything happens to Loretta's horse I can tell you right now you damn sure dont want to be the party that was aboard him.

He handed Wendell one of the lever action rifles he'd brought and swung up into the saddle and pulled his hat down. You ready? he said.

They rode side by side. We've drove all through their tracks but you can still see what it was, Bell said. Big offroad tires.

When they got to the car it was just a blackened hulk.

You were right about the plates, Wendell said.

I lied about the tires though.

How's that.

I said they'd still be burnin.

The car sat in what looked like four puddles of tar, the wheels wrapped in blackened skeins of wire. They rode on. Bell pointed at the ground from time to time. You can tell the day tracks from the night ones, he said. They were drivin out here with no lights. See there how crooked the track is? Like you can just see far enough ahead to duck the brush in front of you. Or you might leave some paint on a rock like that right yonder.

In a sandwash he got down and walked up and back and then looked away toward the south. It's the same tire tread comin back as was goin down. Made about the same time. You can see the sipes real clear. Which way they're a goin. They's two or more trips each way, I'd say.

Wendell sat his horse, his hands crossed on the big roping pommel. He leaned and spat. He looked off to the south with the sheriff. What do you reckon it is we're fixin to find down here?

I dont know, Bell said. He put his foot in the stirrup and stood easily up into the saddle and put the little horse forward. I dont know, he said again. But I cant say as I'm much lookin forward to it.

When they reached Moss's truck the sheriff sat and studied it and then rode slowly around it. Both doors were open.

Somebody's pried the inspection plate off the door, he said.

The numbers is on the frame.

Yeah. I dont think that's why they took it.

I know that truck.

I do too.

Wendell leaned and patted the horse on the neck. The boy's name is Moss.

Yep.

Bell rode back around the rear of the truck and turned the

horse to the south and looked at Wendell. You know where he lives at?

No sir.

He's married, aint he.

I believe he is.

The sheriff sat looking at the truck. I was just thinkin it'd be a curious thing if he was missin two or three days and nobody said nothin about it.

Pretty curious.

Bell looked down toward the caldera. I think we got some real mischief here.

I hear you, Sheriff.

You think this boy's a doperunner?

I dont know. I wouldnt of thought it.

I wouldnt either. Let's go down here and look at the rest of this mess.

They rode down into the caldera carrying the Winchesters upright before them in the saddlebow. I hope this boy aint dead down here, Bell said. He seemed a decent enough boy the time or two I seen him. Pretty wife too.

They rode past the bodies on the ground and stopped and got down and dropped the reins. The horses stepped nervously.

Let's take the horses out yonder a ways, Bell said. They dont need to see this.

Yessir.

When he came back Bell handed him two billfolds he'd taken from the bodies. He looked toward the trucks.

These two aint been dead all that long, he said.

Where they from?

Dallas.

He handed Wendell a pistol he'd picked up and then he squatted and leaned on the rifle he was carrying. These two is been executed, he said. One of their own, I'd say. Old boy never even got the safety off that pistol. Both of em shot between the eyes.

The othern didnt have a gun?

Killer could of took it. Or he might not of had one.

Bad way to go to a gunfight.

Bad way.

They walked among the trucks. These sumbitches are bloody as hogs, Wendell said.

Bell glanced at him.

Yeah, Wendell said. I guess you ought to be careful about cussin the dead.

I would say at the least there probably aint no luck in it.

It's just a bunch of Mexican drugrunners.

They were. They aint now.

I aint sure what you're sayin.

I'm just sayin that whatever they were the only thing they are now is dead.

I'll have to sleep on that.

The sheriff tilted forward the Bronco seat and looked in the rear. He wet his finger and pressed it to the carpet and held his finger to the light. That's been some of that old mexican brown dope in the back of this rig.

Long gone now though, aint it.

Long gone.

Wendell squatted and studied the ground under the door. It looks like there's some more here on the ground. Could be that somebody cut into one of the packages. See what was inside.

Could of been checkin the quality. Gettin ready to trade.

They didnt trade. They shot each other.

Bell nodded.

There might not of even been no money.

That's possible.

But you dont believe it.

Bell thought about it. No, he said. Probably I dont.

There was a second mix-up out here.

Yes, Bell said. At least that.

He rose and pushed the seat back. This good citizen's been shot between the eyes too.

Yep.

They walked around the truck. Bell pointed.

That's been a machinegun, them straight runs yonder.

I'd say it has. So where do you reckon the driver got to?

It's probably one of them layin in the grass yonder.

Bell had taken out his kerchief and he held it across his

nose and reached in and picked up a number of brass shell-casings out of the floor and looked at the numbers stamped in the base.

What calibers you got there, Sheriff?

Nine millimeter. A couple of .45 ACP's.

He dropped the shells back into the floor and stepped back and picked up his rifle from where he'd leaned it against the vehicle. Somebody's unloaded on this thing with a shotgun by the look of it.

You think them holes are big enough?

I dont think they're double ought. More likely number four buck.

More buck for your bang.

You could put it that way. You want to clean out a alley that's a pretty good way to go.

Wendell looked over the caldera. Well, he said. Somebody's walked away from here.

I'd say they have.

How come do you reckon the coyotes aint been at them?

Bell shook his head. I dont know, he said. Supposedly they wont eat a Mexican.

Them over yonder aint Mexican.

Well, that's true.

It must of sounded like Vietnam out here.

Vietnam, the sheriff said.

They walked out between the trucks. Bell picked up a few more casings and looked at them and dropped them again.

He picked up a blue plastic speedloader. He stood and looked over the scene. I'll tell you what, he said.

Tell me.

It dont much stand to reason that the last man never even got hit.

I would agree with that.

Why dont we get the horses and just ride up here a ways and look around. Maybe cut for sign a little.

We can do that.

Can you tell me what they wanted with a dog out here?

I got no idea.

When they found the dead man in the rocks a mile to the northeast Bell just sat his wife's horse. He sat there for a long time.

What are you thinkin, Sheriff?

The sheriff shook his head. He got down and walked over to where the dead man lay slumped. He walked over the ground, the rifle yoked across his shoulders. He squatted and studied the grass.

We got another execution here Sheriff?

No, I believe this one's died of natural causes.

Natural causes?

Natural to the line of work he's in.

He aint got a gun.

No.

Wendell leaned and spat. Somebody's been here before us.

I'd say so.

You think he was packin the money?

I'd say there's a good chance of it.

So we still aint found the last man, have we?

Bell didnt answer. He rose and stood looking out over the country.

It's a mess, aint it Sheriff?

If it aint it'll do till a mess gets here.

They rode back across the upper end of the caldera. They sat the horses and looked down at Moss's truck.

So where do you think this good old boy is at? Wendell said.

I do not know.

I would take it his whereabouts is pretty high on your worklist.

The sheriff nodded. Pretty high, he said.

They drove back to town and the sheriff sent Wendell on to the house with the truck and the horses.

You be sure and rap on the kitchen door and thank Loretta.

I will. I got to give her the keys anyways.

The county dont pay her to use her horse.

I hear you.

He called Torbert on the mobile phone. I'm comin to get you, he said. Just set tight.

When he pulled up in front of Lamar's office the police tape was still strung across the courthouse lawn. Torbert was sitting on the steps. He got up and walked out to the car.

You all right? Bell said.

Yessir.

Where's Sheriff Lamar?

He's out on a call.

They drove out toward the highway. Bell told the deputy about the caldera. Torbert listened in silence. He rode looking out the window. After a while he said: I got the report from Austin.

What do they say.

Not much of anything.

What was he shot with?

They dont know.

They dont know?

No sir.

How can they not know? There wasnt no exit wound.

Yessir. They freely admitted that.

Freely admitted?

Yessir.

Well what the hell did they say, Torbert?

They said that he had what looked to be a large caliber bullet wound in the forehead and that said wound had penetrated to a distance of approximately two and a half inches through the skull and into the frontal lobe of the brain but that there was not no bullet to be found.

Said wound.

Yessir.

Bell pulled out onto the interstate. He drummed his fingers on the steering wheel. He looked at his deputy.

What you're sayin dont make no sense, Torbert.

I told em that.

To which they responded?

They didnt respond nothin. They're sendin the report FedEx. X-rays and everthing. They said you'd have it in your office by in the mornin.

They rode along in silence. After a while Torbert said: This whole thing is just hell in spectacles, aint it Sheriff.

Yes it is.

How many bodies is it altogether?

Good question. I aint sure I even counted. Eight. Nine with Deputy Haskins.

Torbert studied the country out there. The shadows long on the road. Who the hell are these people? he said.

I dont know. I used to say they were the same ones we've always had to deal with. Same ones my grandaddy had to deal with. Back then they was rustlin cattle. Now they're runnin dope. But I dont know as that's true no more. I'm like you. I aint sure we've seen these people before. Their kind. I dont know what to do about em even. If you killed em all they'd have to build a annex on to hell.

Chigurh pulled in to the Desert Aire shortly before noon and parked just below Moss's trailer and shut off the engine. He got out and walked across the raw dirt yard and climbed the steps and tapped at the aluminum door. He waited. Then he tapped again. He turned and stood with his back to the trailer and studied the little park. Nothing moved. Not a dog. He turned and put his wrist to the doorlock and shot out the lock cylinder with the cobalt steel plunger of the cattlegun and opened the door and went in and shut the door behind him.

He stood, the deputy's revolver in his hand. He looked in the kitchen. He walked back into the bedroom. He walked through the bedroom and pushed open the bathroom door and went into the second bedroom. Clothes on the floor. The closet door open. He opened the top dresser drawer and closed it again. He put the gun back in his belt and pulled his shirt over it and walked back out to the kitchen.

He opened the refrigerator and took out a carton of milk and opened it and smelled it and drank. He stood there holding the carton in one hand and looking out the window. He drank again and then he put the carton back in the refrigerator and shut the door.

He went into the livingroom and sat on the sofa. There was a perfectly good twenty-one inch television on the table. He looked at himself in the dead gray screen.

He rose and got the mail off the floor and sat back down and went through it. He folded three of the envelopes and put them in his shirtpocket and then rose and went out.

He drove down and parked in front of the office and went in. Yessir, the woman said.

I'm looking for Llewelyn Moss.

She studied him. Did you go up to his trailer?

Yes I did.

Well I'd say he's at work. Did you want to leave a message?

Where does he work?

Sir I aint at liberty to give out no information about our residents.

Chigurh looked around at the little plywood office. He looked at the woman.

Where does he work.

Sir?

I said where does he work.

Did you not hear me? We cant give out no information.

A toilet flushed somewhere. A doorlatch clicked. Chigurh looked at the woman again. Then he went out and got in the Ramcharger and left.

He pulled in at the cafe and took the envelopes out of his shirtpocket and unfolded them and opened them and read the letters inside. He opened the phone bill and looked at the charges. There were calls to Del Rio and to Odessa.

He went in and got some change and went to the payphone and dialed the Del Rio number but there was no answer. He called the Odessa number and a woman answered and he asked for Llewelyn. The woman said he wasnt there.

I tried to reach him in Sanderson but I dont believe he's there anymore.

There was a silence. Then the woman said: I dont know where he's at. Who is this?

Chigurh hung up the phone and went over to the counter and sat down and ordered a cup of coffee. Has Llewelyn been in? he said.

When he pulled up in front of the garage there were two men sitting with their backs to the wall of the building eating their lunches. He went in. There was a man at the desk drinking coffee and listening to the radio. Yessir, he said.

I was looking for Llewelyn.

He aint here.

What time do you expect him?

I dont know. He aint called in or nothin so your guess is as good as mine. He leaned his head slightly. As if he'd get another look at Chigurh. Is there somethin I can help you with?

I dont think so.

Outside he stood on the broken oilstained pavement. He looked at the two men sitting at the end of the building.

Do you know where Llewelyn is?

They shook their heads. Chigurh got into the Ramcharger and pulled out and went back toward town.

The bus pulled into Del Rio in the early afternoon and Moss got his bags and climbed down. He walked down to the cabstand and opened the rear door of the cab parked there and got in. Take me to a motel, he said.

The driver looked at him in the mirror. You got one in mind?

No. Just someplace cheap.

They drove out to a place called the Trail Motel and Moss got out with his bag and the document case and paid the driver and went into the office. A woman was sitting watching television. She got up and went around behind the desk.

Do you have a room?

I got more than one. How many nights?

I dont know.

We got a weekly rate is the reason I ask. Thirty-five dollars plus a dollar seventy-five tax. Thirty-six seventy-five.

Thirty-six seventy-five.

Yessir.

For the week.

Yessir. For the week.

Is that your best rate?

Yessir. There's not no discounts on the weekly rate.

Well let's just take it one day at a time.

Yessir.

He got the key and walked down to the room and went in and shut the door and set the bags on the bed. He closed the curtains and stood looking out through them at the squalid little court. Dead quiet. He fastened the chain on the door and sat on the bed. He unzipped the duffel bag and took out the machinepistol and laid it on the bedspread and lay down beside it.

When he woke it was late afternoon. He lay there looking at the stained asbestos ceiling. He sat up and pulled off his boots and socks and examined the bandages on his heels. He went into the bathroom and looked at himself in the mirror and he took off his shirt and examined the back of his arm. It was discolored from shoulder to elbow. He walked back into the room and sat on the bed again. He looked at the gun lying there. After a while he climbed up onto the cheap wooden desk and with the blade of his pocketknife set to unscrewing the airduct grille, putting the screws in his mouth one by one. Then he pulled the grille loose and laid it on the desk and stood on his toes and looked into the duct.

He cut a length from the venetian blind cord at the window and tied the end of the cord to the case. Then he unlatched the case and counted out a thousand dollars and folded the money and put it in his pocket and shut the case and fastened it and fastened the straps.

He got the clothes pole out of the closet, sliding the wire hangers off onto the floor, and stood on the dresser again and pushed the case down the duct as far as he could reach. It was a tight fit. He took the pole and pushed it again until he could just reach the end of the rope. He put the grille back with its rack of dust and fastened the screws and climbed down and went into the bathroom and took a shower. When he came out he lay on the bed in his shorts and pulled the chenille spread over himself and over the submachinegun at his side. He pushed the safety off. Then he went to sleep.

When he woke it was dark. He swung his legs over the edge of the bed and sat listening. He rose and walked to the window and pulled the curtain back slightly and looked out. Deep shadows. Silence. Nothing.

He got dressed and put the gun under the mattress with the safety still off and smoothed down the dustskirt and sat on the bed and picked up the phone and called a cab.

He had to pay the driver an extra ten dollars to take him across the bridge to Ciudad Acuña. He walked the streets, looking into the shopwindows. The evening was soft and warm and in the little alameda grackles were settling in the trees and calling to one another. He went into a boot shop and looked at the exotics—crocodile and ostrich and elephant—but the quality of the boots was nothing like the Larry Mahans that he wore. He went into a farmacia and bought a tin of bandages and sat in the park and patched his raw feet. His socks were already bloody. At the corner a cabdriver asked him if he wanted to go see the girls and Moss held up his hand for him to see the ring he wore and kept on walking.

He ate in a restaurant with white tablecloths and waiters in white jackets. He ordered a glass of red wine and a porterhouse steak. It was early and the restaurant was empty save for him. He sipped the wine and when the steak came he cut into it and chewed slowly and thought about his life.

He got back to the motel a little after ten and sat in the cab with the motor running while he counted out money for the fare. He handed the bills across the seat and he started to get out but he didnt. He sat there with his hand on the door-handle. Drive me around to the side, he said.

The driver put the shifter in gear. What room? he said.

Just drive me around. I want to see if somebody's here.

They drove slowly past his room. There was a gap in the curtains he was pretty sure he hadnt left there. Hard to tell. Not that hard. The cab tolled slowly past. No cars in the lot that hadnt been there. Keep going, he said.

The driver looked at him in the mirror.

Keep going, said Moss. Dont stop.

I dont want to get in some kind of a jackpot here, buddy.

Just keep going.

Why dont I let you out here and we wont argue about it.

I want you to take me to another motel.

Let's just call it square.

Moss leaned forward and held a hundred dollar bill across the seat. You're already in a jackpot, he said. I'm tryin to get you out of it. Now take me to a motel.

The driver took the bill and tucked it into his shirtpocket and turned out of the lot and into the street.

He spent the night at the Ramada Inn out on the highway and in the morning he went down and ate breakfast in the diningroom and read the paper. Then he just sat there.

They wouldnt be in the room when the maids came to clean it.

Checkout time is eleven oclock.

They could have found the money and left.

Except of course that there were probably at least two parties looking for him and whichever one this was it wasnt the other and the other wasnt going away either.

By the time he got up he knew that he was probably going to have to kill somebody. He just didnt know who it was.

He took a cab and went into town and went into a sporting goods store and bought a twelve gauge Winchester pump gun and a box of double ought buckshot shells. The box of shells contained almost exactly the firepower of a claymore mine. He had them wrap the gun and he left with it under his arm and walked up Pecan Street to a hardware store. There he bought a hacksaw and a flat millfile and some miscellaneous items. A pair of pliers and a pair of sidecutters. A screwdriver. Flashlight. A roll of duct tape.

He stood on the sidewalk with his purchases. Then he turned and walked back down the street.

In the sporting goods store again he asked the same clerk if he had any aluminum tentpoles. He tried to explain that he didnt care what kind of tent it was, he just needed the poles.

The clerk studied him. Whatever kind of tent it is, he said, we'd still have to special order poles for it. You need to get the manufacturer and the model number.

You sell tents, right?

We got three different models.

Which one has got the most poles in it?

Well, I guess that would be our ten foot walltent. You can stand up in it. Well, some people could stand up in it. It's got a six foot clearance at the ridge.

Let me have one.

Yessir.

He brought the tent from the stockroom and laid it on the counter. It came in an orange nylon bag. Moss laid the shotgun and the bag of hardware on the counter and untied the strings and pulled the tent from the bag together with the poles and cords.

It's all there, the clerk said.

What do I owe you.

It's one seventy-nine plus tax.

He laid two of the hundred dollar bills on the counter. The tentpoles were in a separate bag and he pulled this out and put it with his other things. The clerk gave him his change and the receipt and Moss gathered up the shotgun and his hardware purchases together with the tentpoles and thanked him and turned and left. What about the tent? the clerk called.

In the room he unwrapped the shotgun and wedged it in an open drawer and held it and sawed the barrel off just in front of the magazine. He squared up the cut with the file and smoothed it and wiped out the muzzle of the barrel with a damp facecloth and set it aside. Then he sawed off the stock in a line that left it with a pistol grip and sat on the bed and dressed the grip smooth with the file. When he had it the way he wanted it he slid the forearm back and slid it forward again and let the hammer down with his thumb and turned it sideways and looked at it. It looked pretty good. He turned it over and opened the box of shells and fed the heavy waxed loads into the magazine one by one. He jacked the slide back and chambered a shell and lowered the hammer and then put one more round in the magazine and laid the gun across his lap. It was less than two feet long.

He called the Trail Motel and told the woman to hold his room for him. Then he shoved the gun and the shells and the tools under the mattress and went out again.

He went to Wal-Mart and bought some clothes and a small nylon zipper bag to put them in. A pair of jeans and a couple of shirts and some socks. In the afternoon he went for a long walk out along the lake, taking the cut-off gunbarrel and the stock with him in the bag. He slung the barrel out into the water as far as he could throw it and he buried the stock under a ledge of shale. There were deer moving away through the desert scrub. He heard them snort and he could see them where they came out on a ridge a hundred yards away to stand looking back at him. He sat on a gravel beach with the empty bag folded in his lap and watched the sun set. Watched the land turn blue and cold. An osprey went down the lake. Then there was just the darkness.

IV

I was sheriff of this county when I was twenty-five. Hard to believe. My father was not a lawman. Jack was my grandfather. Me and him was sheriff at the same time, him in Plano and me here. I think he was pretty proud of that. I know I was. I was just back from the war. I had some medals and stuff and of course people had got wind of that. I campaigned pretty hard. You had to. I tried to be fair. Jack used to say that any time you're throwin dirt you're losin ground but I think mostly it just wasnt in him. To speak ill of anybody. And I never did mind bein like him. Me and my wife has been married thirty-one years. No children. We lost a girl but I wont talk about that. I served two terms and then we moved to Denton Texas. Jack used to say that bein sheriff was one of the best jobs you could have and bein a ex-sheriff one of the worst. Maybe lots of things is like that. We stayed gone and stayed gone. I done different things. Was a detective on the railroad for a while. By that time my wife wasnt all that sure about us comin back here. About me runnin. But she seen I wanted to so that's what we done. She's a better person than me, which I will admit to anybody that cares to listen. Not

*that that's sayin a whole lot. She's a better person than any-
body I know. Period.*

*People think they know what they want but they generally
dont. Sometimes if they're lucky they'll get it anyways. Me I
was always lucky. My whole life. I wouldnt be here otherwise. Scrapes I been in. But the day I seen her come out of
Kerr's Mercantile and cross the street and she passed me and I
tipped my hat to her and got just almost a smile back, that
was the luckiest.*

*People complain about the bad things that happen to em
that they dont deserve but they seldom mention the good.
About what they done to deserve them things. I dont recall
that I ever give the good Lord all that much cause to smile on
me. But he did.*

When Bell walked into the cafe on Tuesday morning it was just daylight. He got his paper and went to his table in the corner. The men he passed at the big table nodded to him and said Sheriff. The waitress brought him his coffee and went back to the kitchen and ordered his eggs. He sat stirring the coffee with his spoon although there was nothing to stir since he drank it black. The Haskins boy's picture was on the front page of the Austin paper. Bell read, shaking his head. His wife was twenty years old. You know what you could do for her? Not a damn thing. Lamar had never lost a man in twenty some odd years. This is what he would remember. This is what he'd be remembered for.

She came with his eggs and he folded the paper and laid it by.

He took Wendell with him and they drove down to the Desert Aire and stood at the door while Wendell knocked.

Look at the lock, Bell said.

Wendell drew his pistol and opened the door. Sheriff's department, he called.

There aint nobody here.

No reason not to be careful.

That's right. No reason in the world.

They walked in and stood. Wendell would have holstered his pistol but Bell stopped him. Let's just keep to that careful routine, he said.

Yessir.

He walked over and picked up a small brass slug off of the carpet and held it up.

What's that? said Wendell.

Cylinder out of the lock.

Bell passed his hand over the plywood of the room-divider. Here's where it hit at, he said. He balanced the piece of brass in his palm and looked toward the door. You could weigh this thing and measure the distance and the drop and calculate the speed.

I expect you could.

Pretty good speed.

Yessir. Pretty good speed.

They walked through the rooms. What do you think, Sheriff?

I believe they've done lit a shuck.

I do too.

Kindly in a hurry about it, too.

Yep.

He walked into the kitchen and opened the refrigerator and looked in and shut it again. He looked in the freezer.

So when was he here, Sheriff?

Hard to say. We might of just missed him.

You think this boy has got any notion of the sorts of sons of bitches that are huntin him?

I dont know. He ought to. He seen the same things I seen and it made a impression on me.

They're in a world of trouble, aint they?

Yes they are.

Bell walked back into the livingroom. He sat on the sofa. Wendell stood in the doorway. He was still holding the revolver in his hand. What are you thinkin? he said.

Bell shook his head. He didnt look up.

By Wednesday half of the State of Texas was on its way to Sanderson. Bell sat at his table in the cafe and read the news. He lowered the paper and looked up. A man about thirty years old that he'd never seen before was standing there. He introduced himself as a reporter for the San Antonio Light. What's all this about, Sheriff? he said.

It appears to be a huntin accident.

Hunting accident?

Yessir.

How could it be a hunting accident? You're pulling my leg.

Let me ask you somethin.

All right.

Last year nineteen felony charges were filed in the Terrell County Court. How many of those would you say were not drug related?

I dont know.

Two. In the meantime I got a county the size of Delaware that is full of people who need my help. What do you think about that?

I dont know.

I dont either. Now I just need to eat my breakfast here. I got kindly a full day ahead.

He and Torbert drove out in Torbert's four wheel drive truck. All was as they'd left it. They parked a ways from Moss's truck and waited. It's ten, Torbert said.

What?

It's ten. Deceased. We forgot about old Wyrick. It's ten.

Bell nodded. That we know about, he said.

Yessir. That we know about.

The helicopter arrived and circled and set down in a whirl of dust out on the bajada. Nobody got out. They were waiting for the dust to blow away. Bell and Torbert watched the rotor winding down.

The DEA agent's name was McIntyre. Bell knew him slightly and liked him about well enough to nod to. He got out with a clipboard in his hand and walked toward them. He was dressed in boots and hat and a Carhartt canvas jacket and he looked all right until he opened his mouth.

Sheriff Bell, he said.

Agent McIntyre.

What vehicle is this?

It's a '72 Ford pickup.

McIntyre stood looking out down the bajada. He tapped the clipboard against his leg. He looked at Bell. I'm happy to know that, he said. White in color.

I'd say white. Yes.

Could use a set of tires.

He went over and walked around the truck. He wrote on his clipboard. He looked inside. He folded the seat forward and looked in the back.

Who cut the tires?

Bell was standing with his hands in his back pockets. He leaned and spat. Deputy Hays here believes it was done by a rival party.

Rival party.

Yessir.

I thought these vehicles were all shot up.

They are.

But not this one.

Not this one.

McIntyre looked toward the chopper and he looked down the bajada toward the other vehicles. Can I get a ride down there with you?

Sure you can.

They walked toward Torbert's truck. The agent looked at Bell and he tapped the clipboard against his leg. You dont intend to make this easy, do you?

Hell, McIntyre. I'm just messin with you.

They walked around in the bajada looking at the shot-up

trucks. McIntyre held a kerchief to his nose. The bodies were bloated in their clothes. This is about the damnedest thing I ever saw, he said.

He stood making notes on his clipboard. He paced distances and made a rough sketch of the scene and he copied out the numbers off the license plates.

Were there no guns here? he said.

Not as many as there should of been. We got two pieces in evidence.

How long you think they've been dead?

Four or five days.

Somebody must have got away.

Bell nodded. There's another body about a mile north of here.

There's heroin spilled in the back of that Bronco.

Yep.

Mexican black tar.

Bell looked at Torbert. Torbert leaned and spat.

If the heroin is missing and the money is missing then my guess is that somebody is missing.

I'd say that's a reasonable guess.

McIntyre continued writing. Dont worry, he said. I know you didnt get it.

I aint worried.

McIntyre adjusted his hat and stood looking at the trucks. Are the rangers coming out here?

Rangers are comin. Or one is. DPS drug unit.

I've got .380's, .45's, nine millimeter parabellum, twelve gauge, and .38 special. Did you all find anything else?

I think that was it.

McIntyre nodded. I guess the people waiting for their dope have probably figured out by now that it's not coming. What about the Border Patrol?

Everbody's comin as far as I know. We expect it to get right lively. Might could be a bigger draw than the flood back in '65.

Yeah.

What we need is to get these bodies out of here.

McIntyre tapped the clipboard against his leg. Aint that the truth, he said.

Nine millimeter parabellum, said Torbert.

Bell nodded. You need to put that in your files.

Chigurh picked up the signal from the transponder coming across the high span of the Devil's River Bridge just west of Del Rio. It was near midnight and no cars on the highway. He reached over into the passenger seat and turned the dial slowly forward and then back, listening.

The headlights picked up some kind of a large bird sitting on the aluminum bridgerail up ahead and Chigurh pushed the button to let the window down. Cool air coming in off the lake. He took the pistol from beside the box and cocked and leveled it out the window, resting the barrel on the rearview mirror. The pistol had been fitted with a silencer sweated onto the end of the barrel. The silencer was made out of brass mapp-gas burners fitted into a hairspray can and the whole thing stuffed with fiberglass roofing insulation and painted flat black. He fired just as the bird crouched and spread its wings.

It flared wildly in the lights, very white, turning and lifting away into the darkness. The shot had hit the rail and caromed off into the night and the rail hummed dully in the slipstream and ceased. Chigurh laid the pistol in the seat and put the window back up again.

Moss paid the driver and stepped out into the lights in front of the motel office and slung the bag over his shoulder and shut the cab door and turned and went in. The woman was already behind the counter. He set the bag in the floor and leaned on the counter. She looked a little flustered. Hi, she said. You fixin to stay a while?

I need another room.

You want to change rooms or you want another one besides the one you've got?

I want to keep the one I got and get another one.

All right.

Have you got a map of the motel?

She looked under the counter. There used to be a sort of a one. Wait a minute. I think this is it.

She laid an old brochure on the counter. It showed a car from the fifties parked in front. He unfolded it and flattened it out and studied it.

What about one forty-two?

You can have one next to yours if you want it. One-twenty aint took.

That's all right. What about one forty-two?

She reached and got the key off the board behind her. You'll owe for two nights, she said.

He paid and picked up the bag and walked out and turned down the walkway at the rear of the motel. She leaned over the counter watching him go.

In the room he sat on the bed with the map spread out. He got up and went into the bathroom and stood in the tub with his ear to the wall. A TV was playing somewhere. He went back and sat and unzipped the bag and took out the shotgun and laid it to one side and then emptied the bag out onto the bed.

He took the screwdriver and got the chair from the desk and stood on it and unscrewed the airduct grille and stepped down and laid it dustside up on the cheap chenille bedspread. Then he climbed up and put his ear to the duct. He listened. He stood down and got the flashlight and climbed back up again.

There was a junction in the ductwork about ten feet down the shaft and he could see the end of the bag sticking out. He turned off the light and stood listening. He tried listening with his eyes shut.

He climbed down and got the shotgun and went to the door and turned off the light at the switch there and stood in the dark looking out through the curtain at the courtyard. Then he went back and laid the shotgun on the bed and turned on the flashlight.

He untied the little nylon bag and slid the poles out. They were lightweight aluminum tubes three feet long and he assembled three of them and taped the joints with duct tape so that they wouldnt pull apart. He went to the closet and came back with three wire hangers and sat on the bed and cut the hooks off with the sidecutters and wrapped them into one hook with the tape. Then he taped them to the end of the pole and stood up and slid the pole down the ductwork.

He turned the flashlight off and pitched it onto the bed and went back to the window and looked out. Drone of a truck passing out on the highway. He waited till it was gone. A cat that was crossing the courtyard stopped. Then it went on again.

He stood on the chair with the flashlight in his hand. He turned on the light and laid the lens up close against the gal-vanized metal wall of the duct so as to mute the beam and ran the hook down past the bag and turned it and brought it back. The hook caught and turned the bag slightly and then slipped free again. After a few tries he managed to get it caught in one of the straps and he towed it silently up the duct hand over hand through the dust until he could let go the pole and reach the bag.

He climbed down and sat on the bed and wiped the dust from the case and unfastened the latch and the straps and opened it and looked at the packets of bills. He took one of them from the case and riffled it. Then he fitted it back and undid the length of cord he'd tied to the strap and turned off the flashlight and sat listening. He stood and reached up and shoved the poles down the duct and then he put back the grid and gathered up his tools. He laid the key on the desk and put the shotgun and the tools in the bag and took it and the case and walked out the door leaving everything just as it was.

Chigurh drove slowly along the row of motel rooms with the window down and the receiver in his lap. He turned at the end of the lot and came back. He slowed to a stop and put the Ramcharger in reverse and backed slightly down the blacktop and stopped again. Finally he drove around to the office and parked and went in.

The clock on the motel office wall said twelve forty-two. The television set was on and the woman looked like she'd been asleep. Yessir, she said. Can I help you?

He left the office with the key in his shirtpocket and got into the Ramcharger and drove around to the side of the building and parked and got out and walked down to the room carrying the bag with the receiver and the guns in it. In the room he dropped the bag onto the bed and pulled off his boots and came back out with the receiver and the battery pack and the shotgun from the truck. The shotgun was a twelve gauge Remington automatic with a plastic military stock and a parkerized finish. It was fitted with a shopmade silencer fully a foot long and big around as a beercan. He walked down the ramada in his sockfeet past the rooms listening to the signal.

He came back to the room and stood in the open door under the dead white light from the parking lot lamp. He walked into the bathroom and turned the light on there. He took the measure of the room and looked to see where everything was. He measured where the lightswitches were. Then he stood in the room taking it all in once again. He sat and pulled on his boots and got the airtank and slung it across his shoulder and caught up the cattlegun where it swung from the rubber airhose and walked out and down to the room.

He stood listening at the door. Then he punched out the lock cylinder with the airgun and kicked open the door.

A Mexican in a green guayabera had sat up on the bed and was reaching for a small machinegun beside him. Chigurh shot him three times so fast it sounded like one long gunshot and left most of the upper part of him spread across the headboard and the wall behind it. The shotgun made a strange deep chugging sound. Like someone coughing into a barrel. He snapped on the light and stepped out of the doorway and stood with his back to the outside wall. He looked in again quickly. The bathroom door had been shut. Now it was open. He stepped into the room and fired two loads through the standing door and another through the wall and stepped out again. Down toward the end of the building a light had come on. Chigurh waited. Then he looked into the room once more. The door was blown into shredded plywood hanging off the hinges and a thin stream of blood had started across the pink bathroom tiles.

He stepped into the doorway and fired two more rounds through the bathroom wall and then walked in with the shotgun leveled at his waist. The man was lying slumped against the tub holding an AK-47. He was shot in the chest and the neck and he was bleeding heavily. No me mate, he wheezed. No me mate. Chigurh stepped back to avoid the spray of ceramic chips off the tub and shot him in the face.

He walked out and stood on the sidewalk. No one there. He went back in and searched the room. He looked in the closet and he looked under the bed and he pulled all the drawers out into the floor. He looked in the bathroom. Moss's H&K machinepistol was lying on the sink. He left it there. He wiped his feet back and forth on the carpet to get the blood off the soles of his boots and he stood looking at the room. Then his eye fell on the airduct.

He took the lamp from beside the bed and jerked the cord free and climbed up onto the dresser and stove in the grate with the metal lampbase and pulled it loose and looked in.

He could see the dragmarks in the dust. He climbed down and stood there. He'd got blood and matter on his shirt from off the wall and he took the shirt off and went back into the bathroom and washed himself and dried with one of the bathtowels. Then he wet the towel and wiped off his boots and folded the towel again and wiped down the legs of his jeans. He picked up the shotgun and came back into the room naked to the waist, the shirt balled in one hand. He wiped his bootsoles on the carpet again and looked around the room a last time and left.

When Bell walked into the office Torbert looked up from his desk and then rose and came over and laid a paper down in front of him.

Is this it? Bell said.

Yessir.

Bell leaned back in his chair to read, tapping his lower lip slowly with his forefinger. After a while he put the report down. He didnt look at Torbert. I know what's happened here, he said.

All right.

Have you ever been to a slaughterhouse?

Yessir. I believe so.

You'd know it if you had.

I think I went once when I was a kid.

Funny place to take a kid.

I think I went my own self. Snuck in.

How did they kill the beef?

They had a knocker straddled the chute and they'd let the beeves through one at a time and he'd knock em in the head with a maul. He done that all day.

That sounds about right. They dont do it thataway no more. They use a airpowered gun that shoots a steel bolt out of it. Just shoots it out about so far. They put that thing between the beef's eyes and pull the trigger and down she goes. It's that quick.

Torbert was standing at the corner of Bell's desk. He waited a minute for the sheriff to continue but the sheriff didnt continue. Torbert stood there. Then he looked away. I wish you hadnt of even told me, he said.

I know, said Bell. I knowed what you'd say fore you said it.

Moss pulled into Eagle Pass at a quarter till two in the morning. He'd slept a good part of the way in the back of the cab and he only woke when they slowed coming off the highway and down Main Street. He watched the pale white globes of the streetlamps pass along the upper rim of the window. Then he sat up.

You goin across the river? the driver said.

No. Just take me downtown.

You are downtown.

Moss leaned forward with his elbows on the back of the seat.

What's that right there.

That's the Maverick County Courthouse.

No. Right there where the sign is.

That's the Hotel Eagle.

Drop me there.

He paid the driver the fifty dollars they'd agreed on and picked up his bags off the curb and walked up the steps to the porch and went in. The clerk was standing at the desk as if he'd been expecting him.

He paid and put the key in his pocket and climbed the stairs and walked down the old hotel corridor. Dead quiet. No lights in the transoms. He found the room and put the key in the door and opened it and went in and shut the door behind him. Light from the streetlamps coming through the lace curtains at the window. He set the bags on the bed and went back to the door and switched on the overhead light. Old fashioned pushbutton switchplate. Oak furniture from the turn of the century. Brown walls. Same chenille bedspread.

He sat on the bed thinking things over. He got up and looked out the window at the parking lot and he went into the bathroom and got a glass of water and came back and sat on the bed again. He took a sip and set the water on the glass top of the wooden bedside table. There is no goddamn way, he said.

He undid the brass latch and the buckles on the case and began to take the packets of money out and to stack them on the bed. When the case was empty he checked it for a false bottom and he checked the back and sides and then he set it aside and began to go through the stacks of bills, riffling each of the packets and stacking them back in the case. He'd packed it about a third full before he found the sending unit.

The middle of the packet had been filled in with dollar bills with the centers cut out and the transponder unit nested there was about the size of a Zippo lighter. He slid back the tape and took it out and weighed it in his hand. Then he put it in the drawer and got up and took the cut-out dollar bills and the banktape to the bathroom and flushed them down the toilet and came back. He folded the loose hundreds and put them in his pocket and then packed the rest of the banknotes into the case again and set the case in the chair and sat there looking at it. He thought about a lot of things but the thing that stayed with him was that at some point he was going to have to quit running on luck.

He got the shotgun out of the bag and laid it on the bed and turned on the bedside lamp. He went to the door and turned off the overhead light and came back and stretched out on the bed and stared at the ceiling. He knew what was coming. He just didnt know when. He got up and went into the bathroom and pulled the chain on the light over the sink and looked at himself in the mirror. He took a washcloth from the glass towelbar and turned on the hot water and wet the cloth and wrung it out and wiped his face and the back of his neck. He took a leak and then switched off the light and went back and sat on the bed. It had already occurred to him that he would probably never be safe again in his life and he wondered if that was something that you got used to. And if you did?

He emptied out the bag and put the shotgun in and zipped it shut and took it together with the satchel down to the desk. The Mexican who'd checked him in was gone and in his place was another clerk, thin and gray. A thin white shirt and a black bow tie. He was smoking a cigarette and reading Ring magazine and he looked up at Moss with no great enthusiasm, squinting in the smoke. Yessir, he said.

Did you just come on?

Yessir. Be here till ten in the mornin.

Moss laid a hundred dollar bill on the counter. The clerk put down the magazine.

I aint askin you to do nothin illegal, Moss said.

I'm just waitin to hear your description of that, the clerk said.

There's somebody lookin for me. All I'm askin you to do is to call me if anybody checks in. By anybody I mean any swingin dick. Can you do that?

The nightclerk took the cigarette out of his mouth and held it over a small glass ashtray and tipped the ash from the end of it with his little finger and looked at Moss. Yessir, he said. I can do that.

Moss nodded and went back upstairs.

The phone never rang. Something woke him. He sat up and looked at the clock on the table. Four thirty-seven. He swung his legs over the side of the bed and reached and got his boots and pulled them on and sat listening.

He went over and stood with his ear to the door, the shotgun in one hand. He went in the bathroom and pulled back the plastic showercurtain where it hung on rings over the tub and turned on the tap and pulled the plunger to start the shower. Then he pulled the curtain back around the tub and went out and closed the bathroom door behind him.

He stood at the door listening again. He dragged out the nylon bag from where he'd pushed it under the bed and set it in the chair in the corner. He went over and switched on the light at the bedside table and stood there trying to think. He realized that the phone might ring and he took the receiver from the cradle and laid it on the table. He pulled back the covers and rumpled the pillows on the bed. He looked at the clock. Four forty-three. He looked at the phone lying there on the table. He picked it up and pulled the cord out of it and put it back in the cradle. Then he went over and stood at the door, his thumb on the hammer of the shotgun. He dropped to his stomach and put his ear to the space under the door. A cool wind. As if a door had opened somewhere. What have you done. What have you failed to do.

He went to the far side of the bed and dropped down and pushed himself underneath it and lay there on his stomach with the shotgun pointed at the door. Just space enough beneath the wooden slats. Heart pumping against the dusty carpet. He waited. Two columns of dark intersected the bar of light beneath the door and stood there. The next thing he heard was the key in the lock. Very softly. Then the door opened. He could see out into the hallway. There was no one there. He waited. He tried not even to blink but he did. Then there was an expensive pair of ostrichskin boots standing in the doorway. Pressed jeans. The man stood there. Then he came in. Then he crossed slowly to the bathroom.

At that moment Moss realized that he was not going to open the bathroom door. He was going to turn around. And when he did it would be too late. Too late to make any more mistakes or to do anything at all and that he was going to die. Do it, he said. Just do it.

Dont turn around, he said. You turn around and I'll blow you to hell.

The man didnt move. Moss was walking forward on his elbows holding the shotgun. He could see no higher than the man's waist and he didnt know what kind of gun he was carrying. Drop the gun, he said. Do it now.

A shotgun clattered to the floor. Moss pulled himself up. Get your hands up, he said. Step back from the door.

He took two steps back and stood, his hands at shoulder level. Moss came around the end of the bed. The man was no more than ten feet away. The whole room was pulsing slowly. There was an odd smell in the air. Like some foreign cologne.

A medicinal edge to it. Everything humming. Moss held the shotgun at his waist with the hammer cocked. There was nothing that could happen that would have surprised him. He felt as if he weighed nothing. He felt as if he were floating. The man didnt even look at him. He seemed oddly untroubled. As if this were all part of his day.

Back up. Some more.

He did. Moss picked up the man's shotgun and threw it onto the bed. He switched on the overhead light and shut the door. Look over here, he said.

The man turned his head and gazed at Moss. Blue eyes. Serene. Dark hair. Something about him faintly exotic. Beyond Moss's experience.

What do you want?

He didnt answer.

Moss crossed the room and took hold of the footpost of the bed and swung the bed sideways with one hand. The document case stood there in the dust. He picked it up. The man didnt even seem to notice. His thoughts seemed elsewhere.

He took the nylon bag from the chair and slung it over his shoulder and he got the shotgun with its huge canlike silencer off the bed and put it under his arm and picked up the case again. Let's go, he said. The man lowered his hands and walked out into the hallway.

The small box that held the transponder receiver was standing in the floor just outside the door. Moss left it there. He had the feeling he'd already taken more chances than he had coming. He backed down the hallway with his shotgun trained on the man's belt, holding it in one hand like a pistol. He started to tell him to put his hands back up but something told him that it didnt really make any difference where the man's hands were. The bedroom door was still open, the shower still running.

You show your face at the head of these stairs and I'll shoot you.

The man didnt answer. He could have been a mute for all that Moss knew.

Right there, Moss said. Dont you take another step.

He stopped. Moss backed to the stairs and took one last look at him standing there in the dull yellow light from the wallsconce and then he turned and doubled down the stairwell taking the steps two at a time. He didnt know where he was going. He hadnt thought that far ahead.

In the lobby the nightclerk's feet were sticking out from behind the desk. Moss didnt stop. He pushed out through the front door and down the steps. By the time he'd crossed the street Chigurh was already on the balcony of the hotel above him. Moss felt something tug at the bag on his shoulder. The pistolshot was just a muffled pop, flat and small in the dark quiet of the town. He turned in time to see the muzzleflash of the second shot faint but visible under the pink glow of the fifteen foot high neon hotel sign. He didnt feel anything. The bullet snapped at his shirt and blood started running down his upper arm and he was already at a dead run. With the next shot he felt a stinging pain in his side. He fell down and got up again leaving Chigurh's shotgun lying in the street. Damn, he said. What a shot.

He loped wincing down the sidewalk past the Aztec Theatre. As he passed the little round ticket kiosk all the glass fell out of it. He never even heard that shot. He spun with the shotgun and thumbed back the hammer and fired. The buckshot rattled off the second storey balustrade and took the glass out of some of the windows. When he turned again a car coming down Main Street picked him up in the lights and slowed and then speeded up again. He turned up Adams Street and the car skidded sideways through the intersection in a cloud of rubbersmoke and stopped. The engine had died and the driver was trying to start it. Moss turned with his back to the brick wall of the building. Two men had come from the car and were crossing the street on foot at a run. One of them opened fire with a small caliber machinegun and he fired at them twice with the shotgun and then loped on with the warm blood seeping into his crotch. In the street he heard the car start up again.

By the time he got to Grande Street a pandemonium of gunfire had broken out behind him. He didnt think he could run any more. He saw himself limping along in a storewindow across the street, holding his elbow to his side, the bag slung over his shoulder and carrying the shotgun and the leather document case, dark in the glass and wholly unaccountable. When he looked again he was sitting on the sidewalk. Get up you son of a bitch, he said. Dont you set there and die. You get the hell up.

He crossed Ryan Street with blood sloshing in his boots. He pulled the bag around and unzipped it and shoved the shotgun in and zipped it shut again. He stood tottering. Then he crossed to the bridge. He was cold and shivering and he thought he was going to vomit.

There was a changewindow and a turnstile on the American side of the bridge and he put a dime in the slot and pushed through and staggered out onto the span and eyed the narrow walk ahead of him. Just breaking first light. Dull and gray above the floodplain along the east shore of the river. God's own distance to the far side.

Half way he met a party returning. Four of them, young boys, maybe eighteen, partly drunk. He set the case on the sidewalk and took a pack of the hundreds from his pocket. The money was slick with blood. He wiped it on his trouserleg and peeled off five of the bills and put the rest in his back pocket.

Excuse me, he said. Leaning against the chainlink fence. His bloody footprints on the walk behind him like clues in an arcade.

Excuse me.

They were stepping off the curb into the roadway to go around him.

Excuse me I wondered if you all would sell me a coat.

They didnt stop till they were past him. Then one of them turned. What'll you give? he said.

That man behind you. The one in the long coat.

The one in the long coat stopped with the others.

How much?

I'll give you five hundred dollars.

Bullshit.

Come on Brian.

Let's go, Brian. He's drunk.

Brian looked at them and he looked at Moss. Let's see the money, he said.

It's right here.

Let me see it.

Let me hold the coat.

Let's go, Brian.

You take this hundred and let me hold the coat. Then I'll give you the rest.

All right.

He slipped out of the coat and handed it over and Moss handed him the bill.

What's this on it?

Blood.

Blood?

Blood.

He stood holding the bill in one hand. He looked at the blood on his fingers. What happened to you?

I've been shot.

Let's go, Brian. Goddamn.

Let me have the money.

Moss handed him the bills and unshouldered the zipper bag to the sidewalk and struggled into the coat. The boy folded the bills and put them in his pocket and stepped away.

He joined the others and they went on. Then they stopped. They were talking together and looking back at him. He got the coat buttoned and put his money in the inside pocket and shouldered the bag and picked up the leather case. You all need to keep walkin, he said. I wont tell you twice.

They turned and went on. There were only three of them. He shoved at his eyes with the heel of his hand. He tried to see where the fourth one had gone. Then he realized that there was no fourth one. That's all right, he said. Just keep puttin one foot in front of the other.

When he reached the place where the river actually passed beneath the bridge he stopped and stood looking down at it. The Mexican gateshack was just ahead. He looked back down the bridge but the three were gone. A grainy light to the east. Over the low black hills beyond the town. The water moved beneath him slow and dark. A dog somewhere. Silence. Nothing.

There was a stand of tall carrizo cane growing along the American side of the river below him and he set the zipper bag down and took hold of the case by the handles and swung it behind him and then heaved it over the rail and out into space.

Whitehot pain. He held his side and watched the bag turn slowly in the diminishing light from the bridgelamps and drop soundlessly into the cane and vanish. Then he slid to the pavement and sat there in the puddling blood, his face against the wire. Get up, he said. Damn you, get up.

When he reached the gatehouse there was no one there. He pushed through and into the town of Piedras Negras, State of Coahuila.

He made his way up the street to a small park or zocalo where the grackles in the eucalyptus trees were waking and calling. The trees were painted white to the height of a wainscot and from a distance the park seemed set with white posts arrayed at random. In the center a wrought-iron gazebo or bandstand. He collapsed on one of the iron benches with the bag on the bench beside him and leaned forward holding himself. Globes of orange light hung from the lampstands. The world receding. Across from the park was a church. It seemed far away. The grackles creaked and swayed in the branches overhead and day was coming.

He put out one hand on the bench beside him. Nausea. Dont lie down.

No sun. Just the gray light breaking. The streets wet. The shops closed. Iron shutters. An old man was coming along pushing a broom. He paused. Then he moved on.

Señor, Moss said.

Bueno, the old man said.

You speak english?

He studied Moss, holding the broom handle in both hands. He shrugged his shoulders.

I need a doctor.

The old man waited for more. Moss pushed himself up. The bench was bloody. I've been shot, he said.

The old man looked him over. He clucked his tongue. He looked away toward the dawn. The trees and buildings taking shape. He looked at Moss and gestured with his chin. Puede andar? he said.

What?

Puede caminar? He made walking motions with his fingers, his hand hanging loosely at the wrist.

Moss nodded. A wave of blackness came over him. He waited till it passed.

Tiene dinero? The sweeper rubbed his thumb and fingers together.

Sí, Moss said. Sí. He rose and stood swaying. He took the packet of bloodsoaked bills from the overcoat pocket and separated a hundred dollar note and handed it to the old man. The old man took it with great reverence. He looked at Moss and then he stood the broom against the bench.

When Chigurh came down the steps and out the front door of the hotel he had a towel wrapped around his upper right leg and tied with sections of window blind cord. The towel was already wet through with blood. He was carrying a small bag in one hand and a pistol in the other.

The Cadillac was crossways in the intersection and there was gunfire in the street. He stepped back into the doorway of the barbershop. The clatter of automatic riflefire and the deep heavy slam of a shotgun rattling off the facades of the buildings. The men in the street were dressed in raincoats and tennis shoes. They didnt look like anybody you would expect to meet in this part of the country. He limped back up the steps to the porch and laid the pistol over the balustrade and opened fire on them.

By the time they'd figured out where the fire was coming from he'd killed one and wounded another. The wounded man got behind the car and opened up on the hotel. Chigurh stood with his back to the brick wall and fitted a fresh clip into the pistol. The rounds were taking out the glass in the doors and splintering up the sashwork. The foyer light went out. It was still dark enough in the street that you could see the muzzleflashes. There was a break in the firing and Chigurh turned and pushed his way through into the hotel lobby, the bits of glass crackling under his boots. He went gimping down the hallway and down the steps at the rear of the hotel and out into the parking lot.

He crossed the street and went up Jefferson keeping to the north wall of the buildings, trying to hurry and swinging the bound leg out at his side. All of this was one block from the Maverick County Courthouse and he figured he had minutes at best before fresh parties began to arrive.

When he got to the corner there was only one man standing in the street. He was at the rear of the car and the car was badly shot up, all of the glass gone or shot white. There was at least one body inside. The man was watching the hotel and Chigurh leveled the pistol and shot him twice and he fell down in the street. Chigurh stepped back behind the corner of the building and stood with the pistol upright at his shoulder, waiting. A rich tang of gunpowder on the cool morning air. Like the smell of fireworks. No sound anywhere.

When he limped out into the street one of the men he'd shot from the hotel porch was crawling toward the curb. Chigurh watched him. Then he shot him in the back. The other one was lying by the front fender of the car. He'd been shot through the head and the dark blood was pooled all about him. His weapon was lying there but Chigurh paid it no mind. He walked to the rear of the car and jostled the man there with his boot and then bent and picked up the machinegun he'd been firing. It was a shortbarreled Uzi with the twenty-five round clip. Chigurh rifled the dead man's raincoat pockets and came up with three more clips, one of them full. He put them in the pocket of his jacket and stuck the pistol down in the front of his belt and checked the rounds in the clip that was in the Uzi. Then he slung the piece over his shoulder and hobbled back to the curb. The man he'd shot in the back was lying there watching him. Chigurh looked up the street toward the hotel and the courthouse. The tall palm trees. He looked at the man. The man was lying in a spreading pool of blood. Help me, he said. Chigurh took the pistol from his waist. He looked into the man's eyes. The man looked away.

Look at me, Chigurh said.

The man looked and looked away again.

Do you speak english?

Yes.

Dont look away. I want you to look at me.

He looked at Chigurh. He looked at the new day paling all about. Chigurh shot him through the forehead and then stood watching. Watching the capillaries break up in his eyes. The light receding. Watching his own image degrade in that squandered world. He shoved the pistol in his belt and looked back up the street once more. Then he picked up the bag and slung the Uzi over his shoulder and crossed the street and went limping on toward the hotel parking lot where he'd left his vehicle.

V

We come here from Georgia. Our family did. Horse and wagon. I pretty much know that for a fact. I know they's a lots of things in a family history that just plain aint so. Any family. The stories gets passed on and the truth gets passed over. As the sayin goes. Which I reckon some would take as meanin that the truth cant compete. But I dont believe that. I think that when the lies are all told and forgot the truth will be there yet. It dont move about from place to place and it dont change from time to time. You cant corrupt it any more than you can salt salt. You cant corrupt it because that's what it is. It's the thing you're talkin about. I've heard it compared to the rock—maybe in the bible—and I wouldnt disagree with that. But it'll be here even when the rock is gone. I'm sure they's people would disagree with that. Quite a few, in fact. But I never could find out what any of them did believe.

You always tried to be available for your social events and I would always go to things like cemetery cleanins of course. That was all right. The women would fix dinner on the ground and of course it was a way of campaignin but you were doin somethin for folks that couldnt do it for theirselves. Well, you could be cynical about it I reckon and say that you just didnt want em comin around at night. But I think it goes deeper than that. It is community and it is respect, of course, but the dead have more claims on you than what you might want to admit or even what you might know about and them claims can be very strong indeed. Very strong indeed. You get the feelin they just dont want to turn loose. So any little thing helps, in that respect.

What I was sayin the other day about the papers. Here last week they found this couple out in California they would rent out rooms to old people and then kill em and bury em in the yard and cash their social security checks. They'd torture em first, I dont know why. Maybe their television was broke. Now here's what the papers had to say about that. I quote from the papers. Said: Neighbors were alerted when a man run from the premises wearin only a dogcollar. You cant make up such a thing as that. I dare you to even try.

But that's what it took, you'll notice. All that hollerin and diggin in the yard didnt bring it.

That's all right. I laughed myself when I read it. There aint a whole lot else you can do.

It was almost a three hour drive to Odessa and dark when he got there. He listened to the truckers on the radio. Has he got jurisdiction up here? Come on. Hell if I know. I think if he sees you committin a crime he does. Well I'm a reformed criminal then. You got that right old buddy.

He got a city map at the quickstop and spread it out on the seat of the cruiser while he drank coffee out of a styrofoam cup. He traced his route on the map with a yellow marker from the glovebox and refolded the map and laid it on the seat beside him and switched off the domelight and started the engine.

When he knocked at the door Llewelyn's wife answered it. As she opened the door he took off his hat and he was right away sorry he'd done it. She put her hand to her mouth and reached for the doorjamb.

I'm sorry mam, he said. He's all right. Your husband is all right. I just wanted to talk to you if I could.

You aint lyin to me are you?

No mam. I dont lie.

You drove up here from Sanderson?

Yes mam.

What did you want.

I just wanted to visit with you a little bit. Talk to you about your husband.

Well you cant come in here. You'll scare Mama to death. Let me get my coat.

Yes mam.

They drove down to the Sunshine Cafe and sat in a booth at the rear and ordered coffee.

You dont know where he's at, do you.

No I dont. I done told you.

I know you did.

He took off his hat and laid it in the booth beside him and ran his hand through his hair. You aint heard from him?

No I aint.

Nothin.

Not word one.

The waitress brought the coffee in two heavy white china mugs. Bell stirred his with his spoon. He raised the spoon and looked into the smoking silver bowl of it. How much money did he give you?

She didnt answer. Bell smiled. What did you start to say? he said. You can say it.

I started to say that's some more of your business, aint it.

Why dont you just pretend I aint the sheriff.

And pretend you're what?

You know he's in trouble.

Llewelyn aint done nothin.

It's not me he's in trouble with.

Who's he in trouble with then?

Some pretty bad people.

Llewelyn can take care of hisself.

Do you care if I call you Carla?

I go by Carla Jean.

Carla Jean. Is that all right?

That's all right. You dont care if I keep on callin you Sheriff do you?

Bell smiled. No, he said. That's fine.

All right.

These people will kill him, Carla Jean. They wont quit.

He wont neither. He never has.

Bell nodded. He sipped his coffee. The face that lapped and shifted in the dark liquid in the cup seemed an omen of things to come. Things losing shape. Taking you with them. He set the cup down and looked at the girl. I wish I could say that was in his favor. But I have to say I dont think it is.

Well, she said, he's who he is and he always will be. That's why I married him.

But you aint heard from him in a while.

I didnt expect to hear from him.

Were you all havin problems?

We dont have problems. When we have problems we fix em.

Well, you're lucky people.

Yes we are.

She watched him. How come you to ask me that, she said.

About havin problems?

About havin problems.

I just wondered if you were.

Has somethin happened that you know about and I dont?

No. I could ask you the same thing.

Except I wouldnt tell you.

Yes.

You think he's left me, dont you.

I dont know. Has he?

No. He aint. I know him.

You used to know him.

I know him yet. He aint changed.

Maybe.

But you dont believe that.

Well, I guess in all honesty I would have to say that I never knew nor did I ever hear of anybody that money didnt change. I'd have to say he'd be the first.

Well he'll be the first then.

I hope that's true.

Do you really hope that, Sheriff?

Yes. I do.

He aint been charged with nothin?

No. He aint been charged with nothin.

That dont mean he wont be.

No. It dont. If he lives that long.

Well. He aint dead yet.

I hope that's more comfort to you than it is to me.

He sipped the coffee and set the mug down on the table. He watched her. He needs to turn the money in, he said. They'd put it in the papers. Then maybe these people would leave him alone. I cant guarantee that they will. But they might. It's the only chance he's got.

You could put it in the papers anyway.

Bell studied her. No, he said. I couldnt.

Or wouldnt.

Wouldnt then. How much money is it?

I dont know what you're talkin about.

All right.

You care if I smoke? she said.

I think we're still in America.

She got her cigarettes out and lit one and turned her face and blew the smoke out into the room. Bell watched her. How do you think this is goin to end? he said.

I dont know. I dont know how nothin is goin to end. Do you?

I know how it aint.

Like livin happily ever after?

Somethin like that.

Llewelyn's awful smart.

Bell nodded. You ought to be more worried about him I guess is what I'm sayin.

She took a long pull on the cigarette. She studied Bell. Sheriff, she said, I think I'm probably just about as worried as I need to be.

He's goin to wind up killin somebody. Have you thought about that?

He never has.

He was in Vietnam.

I mean as a civilian.

He will.

She didnt answer.

You want some more coffee?

I'm coffeed out. I didnt want none to start with.

She looked off across the cafe. The empty tables. The night cashier was a boy about eighteen and he was bent over the glass counter reading a magazine. My mama's got cancer, she said. She aint got all that long to live.

I'm sorry to hear that.

I call her mama. She's really my grandmother. She raised me and I was lucky to have her. Well. Lucky dont even say it.

Yes mam.

She never did much like Llewelyn. I dont know why. No reason in particular. He was always good to her. I thought after she got diagnosed she'd be easier to live with but she aint. She's got worse.

How come you live with her?

I dont live with her. I aint that ignorant. This is just temporary.

Bell nodded.

I need to get back, she said.

All right. Have you got a gun?

Yeah. I got a gun. I guess you think I'm just bait settin up here.

I dont know.

But that's what you think.

I cant believe it's all that good a situation.

Yeah.

I just hope you'll talk to him.

I need to think about it.

All right.

I'd die and live in hell forever fore I'd turn snitch on Llewelyn. I hope you understand that.

I do understand that.

I never did learn no shortcuts about things such as that. I hope I never do.

Yes mam.

I'll tell you somethin if you want to hear it.

I want to hear it.

You might think I'm peculiar.

I might.

Or you might think it anyway.

No I dont.

When I got out of high school I was still sixteen and I got a job at Wal-Mart. I didnt know what else to do. We needed the money. What little it was. Anyway, the night before I went down there I had this dream. Or it was like a dream. I think I was still about half awake. But it come to me in this dream or whatever it was that if I went down there that he would find me. At the Wal-Mart. I didnt know who he was or what his name was or what he looked like. I just knew that I'd know him when I seen him. I kept a calendar and marked the days. Like when you're in jail. I mean I aint never been in jail, but like you would probably. And on the ninety-ninth day he walked in and he asked me where sportin goods was at and it was him. And I told him where it was at and he looked at me and went on. And directly he come back and he read my nametag and he said my name and he looked at me and he said: What time do you get off? And that was all she wrote. There was not no question in my mind. Not then, not now, not ever.

That's a nice story, Bell said. I hope it has a nice endin.

It happened just like that.

I know it did. I appreciate you talkin to me. I guess I'd better cut you loose, late as it is.

She stubbed out her cigarette. Well, she said. I'm sorry you come all this way not to do no better than what you done.

Bell picked up his hat and put it on and squared it. Well, he said. You do the best you can. Sometimes things turns out all right.

Do you really care?

About your husband?

About my husband. Yes.

Yes mam. I do. The people of Terrell County hired me to look after em. That's my job. I get paid to be the first one hurt. Killed, for that matter. I'd better care.

You're askin me to believe what you say. But you're the one sayin it.

Bell smiled. Yes mam, he said. I'm the one sayin it. I just hope you'll think about what I did say. I aint makin up a word about the kind of trouble he's in. If he gets killed then I got to live with that. But I can do it. I just want you to think about if you can.

All right.

Can I ask you somethin?

You can ask.

I know you aint supposed to ask a woman her age but I couldnt help but be a bit curious.

That's all right. I'm nineteen. I look younger.

How long have you all been married?

Three years. Almost three years.

Bell nodded. My wife was eighteen when we married. Just had turned. Marryin her makes up for ever dumb thing I ever done. I even think I still got a few left in the account. I think I'm way in the black on that. Are you ready?

She got her purse and rose. Bell picked up the check and squared his hat again and eased up from the booth. She put her cigarettes in her purse and looked at him. I'll tell you somethin, Sheriff. Nineteen is old enough to know that if you have got somethin that means the world to you it's all that more likely it'll get took away. Sixteen was, for that matter. I think about that.

Bell nodded. I aint a stranger to them thoughts, Carla Jean. Them thoughts is very familiar to me.

He was asleep in his bed and it still mostly dark out when the phone rang. He looked at the old radium dial clock on the night table and reached and picked up the phone. Sheriff Bell, he said.

He listened for about two minutes. Then he said: I appreciate you callin me. Yep. It's just out and out war is what it is. I dont know no other name for it.

He pulled up in front of the sheriff's office in Eagle Pass at nine-fifteen in the morning and he and the sheriff sat in the office and drank coffee and looked at the photos taken in the street two blocks away three hours earlier.

There's days I'm in favor of givin the whole damn place back to em, the sheriff said.

I hear you, said Bell.

Dead bodies in the street. Citizens' businesses all shot up. People's cars. Whoever heard of such a thing?

Can we go over and take a look?

Yeah. We can go over.

The street was still roped off but there wasnt much to see.

The front of the Eagle Hotel was all shot up and there was broken glass in the sidewalk down both sides of the street. Tires and glass shot out of the cars and holes in the sheet-metal with the little rings of bare steel around them. The Cadillac had been towed off and the glass in the street swept up and the blood hosed away.

Who was it in the hotel do you reckon?

Some Mexican dopedealer.

The sheriff stood smoking. Bell walked off a ways down the street. He stood. He came back up the sidewalk, his boots grinding in the glass. The sheriff flipped his cigarette into the street. You go up Adams there about a half a block you'll see a blood trail.

Goin yon way, I reckon.

If he had any sense. I think them boys in the car got caught in a crossfire. It looks to me like they was shootin towards the hotel and up the street yonder both.

What do you reckon their car was doin in the middle of the intersection thataway?

I got no idea, Ed Tom.

They walked up to the hotel.

What kind of shellcasins did you all pick up?

Mostly nine millimeter with some shotgun hulls and a few .380's. We got a shotgun and two machineguns.

Fully automatic?

Sure. Why not?

Why not.

They walked up the stairs. The porch of the hotel was covered in glass and the woodwork shot up.

The nightclerk got killed. About as bad a piece of luck as you could have, I reckon. Caught a stray round.

Where'd he catch it?

Right between the eyes.

They walked into the lobby and stood. Somebody had thrown a couple of towels over the blood in the carpet behind the desk but the blood had soaked through the towels. He wasnt shot, Bell said.

Who wasnt shot.

The nightclerk.

He wasnt shot?

No sir.

What makes you say that?

You get the lab report and you'll see.

What are you sayin Ed Tom? That they drilled his brains out with a Black and Decker?

That's pretty close. I'll let you think about it.

Driving back to Sanderson it began to snow. He went to the courthouse and did some paperwork and left just before dark. When he pulled up in the driveway behind the house his wife was looking out from the kitchen window. She smiled at him. The falling snow drifted and turned in the warm yellow light.

They sat in the little diningroom and ate. She'd put on music, a violin concerto. The phone didnt ring.

Did you take it off the hook?

No, she said.

Wires must be down.

She smiled. I think it's just the snow. I think it makes people stop and think.

Bell nodded. I hope it comes a blizzard then.

Do you remember the last time it snowed here?

No, I cant say as I do. Do you?

Yes I do.

When was it.

It'll come to you.

Oh.

She smiled. They ate.

That's nice, Bell said.

What is?

The music. Supper. Bein home.

Do you think she was tellin the truth?

I do. Yes.

Do you think that boy is still alive?

I dont know. I hope he is.

You may never hear another word about any of this.

It's possible. That wouldnt be the end of it though, would it?

No, I guess it wouldnt.

You cant count on em to kill one another off like this on a regular basis. But I expect some cartel will take it over sooner or later and they'll wind up just dealin with the Mexican Government. There's too much money in it. They'll freeze out these country boys. It wont be long, neither.

How much money do you think he has?

The Moss boy?

Yes.

Hard to say. Could be in the millions. Well, not too many millions. He carried it out of there on foot.

Did you want some coffee?

Yes I would.

She rose and went to the sideboard and unplugged the percolator and brought it to the table and poured his cup and sat down again. Just dont come home dead some evenin, she said. I wont put up with it.

I better not do it then.

Do you think he'll send for her?

Bell stirred his coffee. He sat holding the steaming spoon above the cup, then he laid it in the saucer. I dont know, he said. I know he'd be a damn fool if he didnt.

The office was on the seventeenth floor with a view over the skyline of Houston and the open lowlands to the ship channel and the bayou beyond. Colonies of silver tanks. Gas flares, pale in the day. When Wells showed up the man told him to come in and told him to shut the door. He didnt even turn around. He could see Wells in the glass. Wells shut the door and stood with his hands crossed before him at the wrist. The way a funeral director might stand.

The man finally turned and looked at him. You know Anton Chigurh by sight, is that correct?

Yessir, that's correct.

When did you last see him?

November twenty-eighth of last year.

How do you happen to remember the date?

I dont happen to remember it. I remember dates. Numbers.

The man nodded. He was standing behind his desk. The desk was of polished stainless steel and walnut and there wasnt anything on it. Not a picture or a piece of paper. Nothing.

We got a loose cannon here. And we're missing product and we're out a bunch of money.

Yessir. I understand that.

You understand that.

Yessir.

That's good. I'm glad I've got your attention.

Yessir. You have my attention.

The man unlocked a drawer in the desk and took out a steel box and unlocked that and took out a card and closed the box and locked it and put it away again. He held up the card between two fingers and looked at Wells and Wells stepped forward and took it.

You pay your own expenses if I remember correctly.

Yessir.

This account will only give up twelve hundred dollars in any twenty-four hour period. That's up from a thousand.

Yessir.

How well do you know Chigurh.

Well enough.

That's not an answer.

What do you want to know?

The man tapped his knuckles on the desk. He looked up. I'd just like to know your opinion of him. In general. The invincible Mr Chigurh.

Nobody's invincible.

Somebody is.

Why do you say that?

Somewhere in the world is the most invincible man. Just as somewhere is the most vulnerable.

That's a belief that you have?

No. It's called statistics. Just how dangerous is he?

Wells shrugged. Compared to what? The bubonic plague? He's bad enough that you called me. He's a psychopathic killer but so what? There's plenty of them around.

He was in a shoot-out at Eagle Pass yesterday.

A shoot-out?

A shoot-out. People dead in the streets. You dont read the papers.

No sir, I dont.

He studied Wells. You've led something of a charmed life, havent you Mr Wells?

In all honesty I cant say that charm has had a whole lot to do with it.

Yes, the man said. What else.

I guess that's it. Were these Pablo's men?

Yes.

You're sure.

Not in the sense that you mean. But reasonably sure. They werent ours. He killed two other men a couple of days before and those two did happen to be ours. Along with the three at that colossal goatfuck a few days before that. All right?

All right. I guess that will do it.

Good hunting, as we used to say. Once upon a time. In the long ago.

Thank you sir. Can I ask you something?

Sure.

I couldnt come back up in that elevator, could I?

Not to this floor. Why?

I was just interested. Security. Always interesting.

It recodes itself after every trip. A randomly generated five digit number. It doesnt print out anywhere. I dial a number and it reads the code back over the phone. I give it to you and you punch it in. Does that answer your question?

Nice.

Yes.

I counted the floors from the street.

And?

There's a floor missing.

I'll have to look into it.

Wells smiled.

You can see yourself out? the man said.

Yes.

All right.

One other thing.

What is that.

I wondered if I could get my parking ticket validated.

The man cocked his head slightly. This is an attempt at humor I suppose.

Sorry.

Good day, Mr Wells.

Right.

. . .

When Wells got to the hotel the plastic ribbons were gone and the glass and wood had been swept up out of the lobby and the place was open for business. There was plywood nailed over the doors and two of the windows and there was a new clerk standing at the desk where the old clerk had been. Yessir, he said.

I need a room, Wells said.

Yessir. Is it just yourself?

Yes.

And for how many nights would that be.

Probably just the one.

The clerk pushed the pad toward Wells and turned to study the keys hanging on the board. Wells filled out the form. I know you're tired of people asking, he said, but what happened to your hotel?

I'm not supposed to discuss it.

That's all right.

The clerk laid the key on the desk. Will that be cash or credit card?

Cash. How much is it?

Fourteen plus tax.

How much is it. Altogether.

Sir?

I said how much is it altogether. You need to tell me how much it is. Give me a figure. All in.

Yessir. That would be fourteen-seventy.

Were you here when all this took place?

No sir. I only started here yesterday. This is just my second shift.

Then what is it you're not supposed to discuss?

Sir?

What time do you get off?

Sir?

Let me rephrase that. What time is your shift over.

The clerk was tall and thin, maybe Mexican and maybe not. His eyes darted briefly over the lobby of the hotel. As if there might be something out there to help him. I just came on at six, he said. The shift is over at two.

And who comes on at two.

I dont know his name. He was the dayclerk.

He wasnt here the night before last.

No sir. He was the dayclerk.

The man who was on duty the night before last. Where is he?

He's not with us anymore.

Have you got yesterday's paper here?

He backed away and looked under the desk. No sir, he said. I think they threw it out.

All right. Send me up a couple of whores and a fifth of whiskey with some ice.

Sir?

I'm just pulling your leg. You need to relax. They're not coming back. I can pretty near guarantee it.

Yessir. I hope to hell not. I didnt even want to take this job.

Wells smiled and tapped the fiberboard keyfob twice on the marble desktop and went up the stairs.

He was surprised to find the police tape still across both of the rooms. He went on to his own room and set his bag in the chair and got out his shavingkit and went in the bathroom and turned on the light. He brushed his teeth and washed his face and went back into the room and stretched out on the bed. After a while he got up and went to the chair and turned the bag sideways and unzipped a compartment in the bottom and took out a suede leather pistolcase. He unzipped the case and took out a stainless steel .357 revolver and went back to the bed and took off his boots and stretched out again with the pistol beside him.

When he woke it was almost dark. He rose and went to the window and pushed back the old lace curtain. Lights in the street. Long reefs of dull red cloud racked over the darkening western horizon. Roofs in a low and squalid skyline. He put the pistol in his belt and pulled his shirt outside of his trousers to cover it and went out and down the hallway in his sockfeet.

It took him about fifteen seconds to get into Moss's room and he shut the door behind him without disturbing the tape. He leaned against the door and smelled the room. Then he stood there just looking things over.

The first thing he did was to walk carefully over the carpet. When he came across the depression where the bed had been moved he swung the bed out into the room. He knelt and blew at the dust and he studied the nap of the carpet. He rose and picked up the pillows and smelled them and put them back. He left the bed standing quarterwise in the room and walked over to the wardrobe and opened the doors and looked in and closed them again.

He went into the bathroom. He ran his forefinger around the sink. A washcloth and handtowel had been used but not the soap. He ran his finger down the side of the tub and then wiped it along the seam of his trousers. He sat on the edge of the tub and tapped his foot on the tiles.

The other room was number 227. He went in and closed the door and turned and stood. The bed had not been slept in. The bathroom door was open. A bloody towel lay in the floor.

He walked over and pushed the door all the way back. There was a bloodstained washcloth in the sink. The other towel was missing. Bloody handprints. A bloody handprint on the edge of the showercurtain. I hope you havent crawled off in a hole somewhere, he said. I sure would like to get paid.

He was abroad in the morning at first light walking the streets and making notes in his head. The pavement had been hosed off but you could still see bloodstains in the concrete of the walkway where Moss had been shot. He went back to Main Street and started again. Bits of glass in the gutters and along the sidewalks. Some of it windowglass and some of it from curbside automobiles. The windows that had been shot out were boarded up with plywood but you could see the pocks in the brickwork or the teardrop smears of lead that had come down from the hotel. He walked back to the hotel and sat on the steps and looked at the street. The sun was coming up over the Aztec Theatre. Something caught his eye at the second floor level. He got up and walked down and crossed the street and climbed the stairs. Two bulletholes in the windowglass. He tapped at the door and waited. Then he opened the door and went in.

A darkened room. Faint smell of rot. He stood until his eyes were accustomed to the dimness. A parlor. A pianola or small organ against the far wall. A chifforobe. A rockingchair by the window where an old woman sat slumped.

Wells stood over the woman studying her. She'd been shot through the forehead and had tilted forward leaving part of the back of her skull and a good bit of dried brainmatter stuck to the slat of the rocker behind her. She had a newspaper in her lap and she was wearing a cotton robe that was black with dried blood. It was cold in the room. Wells looked around. A second shot had marked a date on a calendar on the wall behind her that was three days hence. You could not help but notice. He looked around the rest of the room. He took a small camera from his jacket pocket and took a couple of pictures of the dead woman and put the camera back in his pocket again. Not what you had in mind at all, was it darling? he told her.

Moss woke in a ward with sheeting hung between him and the bed to his left. A shadowshow of figures there. Voices in spanish. Dim noises from the street. A motorcycle. A dog. He turned his face on the pillow and looked into the eyes of a man sitting on a metal chair against the wall holding a bouquet of flowers. How are you feeling? the man said.

I've felt better. Who are you?

My name is Carson Wells.

Who are you?

I think you know who I am. I brought you some flowers.

Moss turned his head and lay staring at the ceiling. How many of you people are there?

Well, I'd say there's only one you've got to worry about right now.

You.

Yes.

What about that guy that come to the hotel.

We can talk about him.

Talk then.

I can make him go away.

I can do that myself.

I dont think so.

You're entitled to your opinions.

If Acosta's people hadnt shown up when they did I dont think you would have made out so good.

I didnt make out so good.

Yes you did. You made out extremely well.

Moss turned his head and looked at the man again. How long have you been here?

About an hour.

Just settin there.

Yes.

You dont have much to do, do you?

I like to do one thing at a time, if that's what you mean.

You look dumbern hell settin there.

Wells smiled.

Why dont you put them damn flowers down.

All right.

He rose and laid the bouquet on the bedside table and sat back in the chair again.

Do you know what two centimeters is?

Yeah. It's a measurement.

It's about three quarters of an inch.

All right.

That's the distance that round missed your liver by.

Is that what the doctor told you?

Yes. You know what the liver does?

No.

It keeps you alive. Do you know who the man is who shot you?

Maybe he didnt shoot me. Maybe it was one of the Mexicans.

Do you know who the man is?

No. Am I supposed to?

Because he's not somebody you really want to know. The people he meets tend to have very short futures. Nonexistent, in fact.

Well good for him.

You're not listening. You need to pay attention. This man wont stop looking for you. Even if he gets the money back. It wont make any difference to him. Even if you went to him and gave him the money he would still kill you. Just for having inconvenienced him.

I think I done a little more than inconvenience him.

How do you mean.

I think I hit him.

Why do you think that?

I sprayed double ought buckshot all over him. I cant believe it done him a whole lot of good.

Wells sat back in the chair. He studied Moss. You think you killed him?

I dont know.

Because you didnt. He came out into the street and killed every one of the Mexicans and then went back into the hotel. Like you might go out and get a paper or something.

He didnt kill ever one of them.

He killed the ones that were left.

You tellin me he wasnt hit?

I dont know.

You mean why would you tell me.

If you like.

Is he a buddy of yours?

No.

I thought maybe he was a buddy of yours.

No you didnt. How do you know he's not on his way to Odessa?

Why would he go to Odessa?

To kill your wife.

Moss didnt answer. He lay on the rough linen looking at the ceiling. He was in pain and it was getting worse. You dont know what the hell you're talkin about, he said.

I brought you a couple of photographs.

He rose and laid two photos on the bed and sat back down again. Moss glanced at them. What am I supposed to make of that? he said.

I took those pictures this morning. The woman lived in an apartment on the second floor of one of the buildings you shot up. The body's still there.

You're full of shit.

Wells studied him. He turned and looked out the window. You dont have anything to do with any of this, do you?

No.

You just happened to find the vehicles out there.

I dont know what you're talkin about.

You didnt take the product, did you?

What product.

The heroin. You dont have it.

No. I dont have it.

Wells nodded. He looked thoughtful. Maybe I should ask you what you intend to do.

Maybe I should ask you.

I dont intend to do anything. I dont have to. You'll come to me. Sooner or later. You dont have a choice. I'm going to give you my mobile phone number.

What makes you think I wont just disappear?

Do you know how long it took me to find you?

No.

About three hours.

You might not get so lucky again.

No, I might not. But that wouldnt be good news for you.

I take it you used to work with him.

Who.

This guy.

Yes. I did. At one time.

What's his name.

Chigurh.

Sugar?

Chigurh. Anton Chigurh.

How do you know I wont cut a deal with him?

Wells sat bent forward in the chair with his forearms across his knees, his fingers laced together. He shook his head. You're not paying attention, he said.

Maybe I just dont believe what you say.

Yes you do.

Or I might take him out.

Are you in a lot of pain?

Some. Yeah.

You're in a lot of pain. It makes it hard to think. Let me get the nurse.

I dont need you to do me no favors.

All right.

What is he supposed to be, the ultimate bad-ass?

I dont think that's how I would describe him.

How would you describe him.

Wells thought about it. I guess I'd say that he doesnt have a sense of humor.

That aint a crime.

That's not the point. I'm trying to tell you something.

Tell me.

You cant make a deal with him. Let me say it again. Even if you gave him the money he'd still kill you. There's no one alive on this planet that's ever had even a cross word with him. They're all dead. These are not good odds. He's a peculiar man. You could even say that he has principles. Principles that transcend money or drugs or anything like that.

So why would you tell me about him.

You asked about him.

Why would you tell me.

I guess because I think if I could get you to understand the position you're in it would make my job easier. I dont know anything about you. But I know you're not cut out for this. You think you are. But you're not.

We'll see, wont we?

Some of us will. What did you do with the money?

I spent about two million dollars on whores and whiskey and the rest of it I just sort of blew it in.

Wells smiled. He leaned back in the chair and crossed his legs. He wore an expensive pair of Lucchese crocodile boots. How do you think he found you?

Moss didnt answer.

Have you thought about that?

I know how he found me. He wont do it again.

Wells smiled. Well good on you, he said.

Yeah. Good on me.

There was a pitcher of water on a plastic tray on the bedside table. Moss no more than glanced at it.

Do you want some water? Wells said.

If I want somethin from you you'll be the first son of a bitch to know about it.

It's called a transponder, Wells said.

I know what it's called.

It's not the only way he has of finding you.

Yeah.

I could tell you some things that would be useful for you to know.

Well, I go back to what I just said. I dont need no favors.

You're not curious to know why I'd tell you?

I know why you'd tell me.

Which is?

You'd rather deal with me than with this sugar guy.

Yes. Let me get you some water.

You go to hell.

Wells sat quietly with his legs crossed. Moss looked at him. You think you can scare me with this guy. You dont know what you're talkin about. I'll take you out with him if that's what you want.

Wells smiled. He gave a little shrug. He looked down at the toe of his boot and uncrossed his legs and passed the toe under his jeans to dust it and recrossed his legs again. What do you do? he said.

What?

What do you do.

I'm retired.

What did you do before you retired?

I'm a welder.

Acetylene? Mig? Tig?

Any of it. If it can be welded I can weld it.

Cast iron?

Yes.

I dont mean braze.

I didnt say braze.

Pot metal?

What did I say?

Were you in Nam?

Yeah. I was in Nam.

So was I.

So what does that make me? Your buddy?

I was in special forces.

I think you have me confused with somebody who gives a shit what you were in.

I was a lieutenant colonel.

Bullshit.

I dont think so.

And what do you do now.

I find people. Settle accounts. That sort of thing.

You're a hit man.

Wells smiled. A hit man.

Whatever you call it.

The sort of people I contract with like to keep a low profile. They dont like to get involved in things that draw attention. They dont like things in the paper.

I'll bet.

This isnt going to go away. Even if you got lucky and took out one or two people–which is unlikely–they'd just send someone else. Nothing would change. They'll still find you. There's nowhere to go. You can add to your troubles the fact that the people who were delivering the product dont have that either. So guess who they're looking at? Not to mention the DEA and various other law enforcement agencies. Everybody's list has got the same name on it. And it's the only name on it. You need to throw me a bone. I dont really have any reason to protect you.

Are you afraid of this guy?

Wells shrugged. Wary is the word I'd use.

You didnt mention Bell.

Bell. All right?

I take it you dont think much of him.

I dont think of him at all. He's a redneck sheriff in a hick town in a hick county. In a hick state. Let me get the nurse. You're not very comfortable. This is my number. I want you to think it over. What we talked about.

He stood and put a card on the table next to the flowers. He looked at Moss. You think you wont call me but you will. Just dont wait too long. That money belongs to my client. Chigurh is an outlaw. Time's not on your side. We can even let you keep some of it. But if I have to recover the funds from Chigurh then it will be too late for you. Not to mention your wife.

Moss didnt answer.

All right. You might want to call her. When I talked to her she sounded pretty worried.

When he was gone Moss turned up the photographs lying on the bed. Like a player checking his hole cards. He looked at the pitcher of water but then the nurse came in.

VI

Young people anymore they seem to have a hard time growin up. I dont know why. Maybe it's just that you dont grow up any faster than what you have to. I had a cousin was a deputized peace officer when he was eighteen. He was married and had a kid at the time. I had a friend that I grew up with was a ordained Baptist preacher at the same age. Pastor of a little old country church. He left there to go to Lubbock after about three years and when he told em he was leavin they just set there in that church and blubbered. Men and women alike. He'd married em and baptized em and buried em. He was twenty-one years old, maybe twenty-two. When he preached they'd be standin out in the yard listenin. It surprised me. He was always quiet in school. I was twenty-one when I went in the army and I was one of the oldest in our class at boot camp. Six months later I was in France shootin people with a rifle. I didnt even think it was all that peculiar at the time. Four years later I was sheriff of this county. I never doubted but what I was supposed to be neither. People anymore you talk about right and wrong they're liable to smile at you. But I never had a lot of doubts about things like that. In my thoughts about things like that. I hope I never do.

Loretta told me that she had heard on the radio about some percentage of the children in this country bein raised by their grandparents. I forget what it was. Pretty high, I thought. Parents wouldnt raise em. We talked about that. What we thought was that when the next generation come along and they dont want to raise their children neither then who is goin to do it? Their own parents will be the only grandparents around and they wouldnt even raise them. We didnt have a answer about that. On my better days I think that there is somethin I dont know or there is somethin that I'm leavin out. But them times are seldom. I wake up sometimes way in the night and I know as certain as death that there aint nothin short of the second comin of Christ that can slow this train. I dont know what is the use of me layin awake over it. But I do.

I dont believe you could do this job without a wife. A pretty unusual wife at that. Cook and jailer and I dont know what all. Them boys dont know how good they've got it. Well, maybe they do. I never worried about her bein safe. They get fresh garden stuff a good part of the year. Good cornbread. Soupbeans. She's been known to fix em hamburgers and french fries. We've had em to come back even years later and they'd be married and doin good. Bring their wives. Bring their kids even. They didnt come back to see me. I've seen em to introduce their wives or their sweethearts and then just go to bawlin. Grown men. That had done some pretty bad things. She knew what she was doin. She always did. So we go over budget on the jail ever month but what are you goin to do about that? You aint goin to do nothin about it. That's what you're goin to do.

Chigurh pulled off of the highway at the junction of 131 and opened the telephone directory in his lap and folded over the bloodstained pages till he got to veterinarian. There was a clinic outside Bracketville about thirty minutes away. He looked at the towel around his leg. It was soaked through with blood and blood had soaked into the seat. He threw the directory in the floor and sat with his hands at the top of the steering wheel. He sat there for about three minutes. Then he put the vehicle in gear and pulled out onto the highway again.

He drove to the crossroads at La Pryor and took the road north to Uvalde. His leg was throbbing like a pump. On the highway outside of Uvalde he pulled up in front of the Cooperative and undid the sashcord from around his leg and pulled away the towel. Then he got out and hobbled in.

He bought a sack full of veterinary supplies. Cotton and tape and gauze. A bulb syringe and a bottle of hydrogen peroxide. A pair of forceps. Scissors. Some packets of four inch swabs and a quart bottle of Betadine. He paid and went out and got in the Ramcharger and started the engine and then sat watching the building in the rearview mirror. As if he might be thinking of something else he needed, but that wasnt it. He put his fingers inside the cuff of his shirt and carefully blotted the sweat from his eyes. Then he put the vehicle in gear and backed out of the parking space and pulled out onto the highway headed toward town.

He drove down Main Street and turned north on Getty and east again on Nopal where he parked and shut off the engine. His leg was still bleeding. He got the scissors from the bag and the tape and he cut a three inch round disc out of the cardboard box that held the cotton. He put that together with the tape into his shirtpocket. He took a coathanger from the floor behind the seat and twisted the ends off and straightened it out. Then he leaned and opened his bag and took out a shirt and cut off one sleeve with the scissors and folded it and put it in his pocket and put the scissors back in the paper bag from the Cooperative and opened the door and eased himself down, lifting his injured leg out with both hands under his knee. He stood there, holding on to the door. Then he bent over with his head to his chest and stood that way for the better part of a minute. Then he raised up and shut the door and started down the street.

Outside the drugstore on Main he stopped and turned and leaned against a car parked there. He checked the street. No one coming. He unscrewed the gascap at his elbow and hooked the shirtsleeve over the coathanger and ran it down into the tank and drew it out again. He taped the cardboard over the open gastank and balled the sleeve wet with gasoline over the top of it and taped it down and lit it and turned and limped into the drugstore. He was little more than half way down the aisle toward the pharmacy when the car outside exploded into flame taking out most of the glass in front of the store.

He let himself in through the little gate and went down the pharmacist's aisles. He found a packet of syringes and a bottle of Hydrocodone tablets and he came back up the aisle looking for penicillin. He couldnt find it but he found tetracycline and sulfa. He stuffed these things in his pocket and came out from behind the counter in the orange glow of the fire and went down the aisle and picked up a pair of aluminum crutches and pushed open the rear door and went hobbling out across the gravel parking lot behind the store. The alarm at the rear door went off but no one paid any attention and Chigurh never had even glanced toward the front of the store which was now in flames.

He pulled into a motel outside of Hondo and got a room at the end of the building and walked in and set his bag on the bed. He shoved the pistol under the pillow and went in the bathroom with the bag from the Cooperative and dumped the contents out into the sink. He emptied his pockets and laid out everything on the counter—keys, billfold, the vials of antibiotic and the syringes. He sat on the edge of the tub and pulled off his boots and reached down and put the plug in the tub and turned on the tap. Then he undressed and eased himself into the tub while it filled.

His leg was black and blue and swollen badly. It looked like a snakebite. He laved water over the wounds with a washcloth. He turned his leg in the water and studied the exit wound. Small pieces of cloth stuck to the tissue. The hole was big enough to put your thumb in.

When he climbed out of the tub the water was a pale pink and the holes in his leg were still leaking a pale blood dilute with serum. He dropped his boots in the water and patted himself dry with the towel and sat on the toilet and took the bottle of Betadine and the packet of swabs from the sink. He tore open the packet with his teeth and unscrewed the bottle and tipped it slowly over the wounds. Then he set the bottle down and bent to work, picking out the bits of cloth, using the swabs and the forceps. He sat with the water running in the sink and rested. He held the tip of the forceps under the faucet and shook away the water and bent to his work again.

When he was done he disinfected the wound a final time and tore open packets of four by fours and laid them over the holes in his leg and bound them with gauze off of a roll packaged for sheep and goats. Then he rose and filled the plastic tumbler on the sink counter with water and drank it. He filled it and drank twice more. Then he went back into the bedroom and stretched out on the bed with his leg propped on the pillows. Other than a light beading of sweat on his forehead there was little evidence that his labors had cost him anything at all.

When he went back into the bathroom he stripped one of the syringes out of the plastic wrapper and sank the needle through the seal into the vial of tetracycline and drew the glass barrel full and held it to the light and pressed the plunger with his thumb until a small bead appeared at the tip of the needle. Then he snapped the syringe twice with his finger and bent and slid the needle into the quadriceps of his right leg and slowly depressed the plunger.

He stayed in the motel for five days. Hobbling down to the cafe on the crutches for his meals and back again. He kept the television on and he sat up in the bed watching it and he never changed channels. He watched whatever came on. He watched soap operas and the news and talk shows. He changed the dressing twice a day and cleaned the wounds with epsom salt solution and took the antibiotics. When the maid came the first morning he went to the door and told her he did not need any service. Just towels and soap. He gave her ten dollars and she took the money and stood there uncertainly. He told her the same thing in spanish and she nodded and put the money in her apron and pushed her cart back up the walkway and he stood there and studied the cars in the parking lot and then shut the door.

On the fifth night while he was sitting in the cafe two deputies from the Valdez County Sheriff's Office came in and sat down and removed their hats and put them in the empty chairs at either side and took the menus from the chrome holder and opened them. One of them looked at him. Chigurh watched it all without turning or looking. They spoke. Then the other one looked at him. Then the waitress came. He finished his coffee and rose and left the money on the table and walked out. He'd left the crutches in the room and he walked slowly and evenly along the walkway past the cafe window trying not to limp. He walked past his room to the end of the ramada and turned. He looked at the Ramcharger parked at the end of the lot. It could not be seen from the office or from the restaurant. He went back to the room and put his shavingkit and the pistol in his bag and walked out across the parking lot and got into the Ramcharger and started it and drove over the concrete divider into the parking lot of the electronics shop next door and out onto the highway.

Wells stood on the bridge with the wind off the river tousling his thin and sandy hair. He turned and leaned against the fence and raised the small cheap camera he carried and took a picture of nothing in particular and lowered the camera again. He was standing where Moss had stood four nights ago. He studied the blood on the walk. Where it trailed off to nothing he stopped and stood with his arms folded and his chin in his hand. He didnt bother to take a picture. There was no one watching. He looked out downriver at the slow green water. He walked a dozen steps and came back. He stepped into the roadway and crossed to the other side. A truck passed. A light tremor in the superstructure. He went on along the walkway and then he stopped. Faint outline of a bootprint in blood. Fainter of another. He studied the chain-link fence to see if there might be blood on the wire. He took his handkerchief from his pocket and wet it with his tongue and passed it among the diamonds. He stood looking down at the river. A road down there along the American side. Between the road and the river a thick stand of carrizo cane. The cane lashed softly in the wind off the river. If he'd carried the money into Mexico it was gone. But he hadnt.

Wells stood back and looked at the bootprints again. Some Mexicans were coming along the bridge with their baskets and dayparcels. He took out his camera and snapped a picture of the sky, the river, the world.

Bell sat at the desk signing checks and totting up figures on a hand calculator. When he was done he leaned back in his chair and looked out the window at the bleak courthouse lawn. Molly, he said.

She came and stood in the door.

Did you find anything on any of those vehicles yet?

Sheriff I found out everything there was to find. Those vehicles are titled and registered to deceased people. The owner of that Blazer died twenty years ago. Did you want me to see what I could find out about the mexican ones?

No. Lord no. Here's your checks.

She came in and took the big leatherette checkbook off his desk and put it under her arm. That DEA agent called again. You dont want to talk to him?

I'm goin to try and keep from it as much as I can.

He said he's goin back out there and he wanted to know if you wanted to go with him.

Well that's cordial of him. I guess he can go wherever he wants. He's a certified agent of the United States Government.

He wanted to know what you were goin to do with the vehicles.

Yeah. I've got to try and sell them things at auction. More county money down the toilet. One of em has got a hot engine in it. We might be able to get a few dollars for that. No word from Mrs Moss?

No sir.

All right.

He looked at the clock on the outer office wall. I wonder if I could get you to call Loretta and tell her I've gone to Eagle Pass and I'll call her from down there. I'd call her but she'll want me to come home and I just might.

You want me to wait till you've quit the buildin?

Yes I do.

He pushed the chair back and rose and got down his gunbelt from the coatrack behind his desk and hung it over his shoulder and picked up his hat and put it on. What is it that Torbert says? About truth and justice?

We dedicate ourselves anew daily. Somethin like that.

I think I'm goin to commence dedicatin myself twice daily. It may come to three fore it's over. I'll see you in the mornin.

He stopped at the cafe and got a coffee to go and walked out to the cruiser as the flatbed was coming up the street. Powdered over with the gray desert dust. He stopped and watched it and then got in the cruiser and wheeled around and drove past the truck and pulled it over. When he got out and walked back the driver was sitting at the wheel chewing gum and watching him with a sort of goodnatured arrogance.

Bell put one hand on the cab and looked in at the driver. The driver nodded. Sheriff, he said.

Have you looked at your load lately?

The driver looked in the mirror. What's the problem, Sheriff?

Bell stepped back from the truck. Step out here, he said.

The man opened the door and got out. Bell nodded toward the bed of the truck. That's a damned outrage, he said.

The man walked back and took a look. One of the tiedowns is worked loose, he said.

He got hold of the loose corner of the tarp and pulled it back up along the bed of the truck over the bodies lying there, each wrapped in blue reinforced plastic sheeting and bound with tape. There were eight of them and they looked like just that. Dead bodies wrapped and taped.

How many did you leave with? Bell said.

I aint lost none of em, Sheriff.

Couldnt you all of took a van out there?

We didnt have no van with four wheel drive.

He tied down the corner of the tarp and stood.

All right, Bell said.

You aint goin to write me up for improperly secured load?

You get your ass out of here.

He reached the Devil's River Bridge at sundown and half way across he pulled the cruiser to a halt and turned on the rooflights and got out and shut the door and walked around in front of the vehicle and stood leaning on the aluminum pipe that served for the top guardrail. Watching the sun set into the blue reservoir beyond the railroad bridge to the west. A westbound semi coming around the long curve of the span downshifted when the lights came into view. The driver leaned from the window as he passed. Dont jump, Sheriff. She aint worth it. Then he was gone in a long suck of wind, the diesel engine winding up and the driver double clutching and shifting gears. Bell smiled. Truth of the matter is, he said, she is.

Some two miles past the junction of 481 and 57 the box sitting in the passenger seat gave off a single bleep and went silent again. Chigurh pulled onto the shoulder and stopped. He picked up the box and turned it and turned it back. He adjusted the knobs. Nothing. He pulled out onto the highway again. The sun pooled in the low blue hills before him. Bleeding slowly away. A cool and shadowed twilight falling over the desert. He took off his sunglasses and put them in the glovebox and closed the glovebox door and turned on the headlights. As he did so the box began to beep with a slow measured time.

He parked behind the hotel and got out and came limping around the truck with the box and the shotgun and the pistol all in a zipper bag and crossed the parking lot and climbed the hotel steps.

He registered and got the key and hobbled up the steps and down the hall to his room and went in and locked the door and lay on the bed with the shotgun across his chest staring at the ceiling. He could think of no reason for the transponder sending unit to be in the hotel. He ruled out Moss because he thought Moss was almost certainly dead. That left the police. Or some agent of the Matacumbe Petroleum Group. Who must think that he thought that they thought that he thought they were very dumb. He thought about that.

When he woke it was ten-thirty at night and he lay there in the half dark and the quiet but he knew what the answer was. He got up and put the shotgun behind the pillows and stuck the pistol into the waistband of his trousers. Then he went out and limped down the stairs to the desk.

The clerk was sitting reading a magazine and when he saw Chigurh he stuck the magazine under the desk and rose. Yessir, he said.

I'd like to see the registration.

Are you a police officer?

No. I'm not.

I'm afraid I cant do that sir.

Yes you can.

When he came back up he stopped and stood listening in the hallway outside his door. He went in and got the shotgun and the receiver and then walked down to the room with the tape across it and held the box to the door and turned it on. He went down to the second door and tried the reception there. Then he came back to the first room and opened the door with the key from the desk and stepped back and stood against the hallway wall.

He could hear traffic in the street beyond the parking lot but still he thought the window was closed. There was no air moving. He looked quickly into the room. Bed pulled away from the wall. Bathroom door open. He checked the safety on the shotgun. He stepped across the doorway to the other side.

There was no one in the room. He scanned the room with the box and found the sending unit in the drawer of the bed-side table. He sat on the bed turning it in his hand. Small lozenge of burnished metal the size of a domino. He looked out the window at the parking lot. His leg hurt. He put the piece of metal in his pocket and turned off the receiver and rose and left, pulling the door shut behind him. Inside the room the phone rang. He thought about that for a minute. Then he set the transponder on the windowsill in the hallway and turned and went back down to the lobby.

And there he waited for Wells. No one would do that. He sat in a leather armchair pushed back into the corner where he could see both the front door and the hallway to the rear. Wells came in at eleven-thirteen and Chigurh rose and followed him up the stairs, the shotgun wrapped loosely in the newspaper he'd been reading. Halfway up the stairs Wells turned and looked back and Chigurh let the paper fall and raised the shotgun to his waist. Hello, Carson, he said.

They sat in Wells' room, Wells on the bed and Chigurh in the chair by the window. You dont have to do this, Wells said. I'm a daytrader. I could just go home.

You could.

I'd make it worth your while. Take you to an ATM. Everybody just walks away. There's about fourteen grand in it.

Good payday.

I think so.

Chigurh looked out the window, the shotgun across his knee. Getting hurt changed me, he said. Changed my perspective. I've moved on, in a way. Some things have fallen into place that were not there before. I thought they were, but they werent. The best way I can put it is that I've sort of caught up with myself. That's not a bad thing. It was overdue.

It's still a good payday.

It is. It's just in the wrong currency.

Wells eyed the distance between them. Senseless. Maybe twenty years ago. Probably not even then. Do what you have to do, he said.

Chigurh sat slouched casually in the chair, his chin resting against his knuckles. Watching Wells. Watching his last thoughts. He'd seen it all before. So had Wells.

It started before that, he said. I didnt realize it at the time. When I went down on the border I stopped in a cafe in this town and there were some men in there drinking beer and one of them kept looking back at me. I didnt pay any attention to him. I ordered my dinner and ate. But when I walked up to the counter to pay the check I had to go past them and they were all grinning and he said something that was hard to ignore. Do you know what I did?

Yeah. I know what you did.

I ignored him. I paid my bill and I had started to push through the door when he said the same thing again. I turned and looked at him. I was just standing there picking my teeth with a toothpick and I gave him a little gesture with my head. For him to come outside. If he would like to. And then I went out. And I waited in the parking lot. And he and his friends came out and I killed him in the parking lot and then I got into my car. They were all gathered around him. They didnt know what had happened. They didnt know that he was dead. One of them said that I had put a sleeper hold on him and then the others all said that. They were trying to get him to sit up. They were slapping him and trying to get him to sit up. An hour later I was pulled over by a sheriff's deputy outside of Sonora Texas and I let him take me into town in handcuffs. I'm not sure why I did this but I think I wanted to see if I could extricate myself by an act of will. Because I believe that one can. That such a thing is possible. But it was a foolish thing to do. A vain thing to do. Do you understand?

Do I understand?

Yes.

Do you have any notion of how goddamned crazy you are?

The nature of this conversation?

The nature of you.

Chigurh leaned back. He studied Wells. Tell me something, he said.

What.

If the rule you followed led you to this of what use was the rule?

I dont know what you're talking about.

I'm talking about your life. In which now everything can be seen at once.

I'm not interested in your bullshit, Anton.

I thought you might want to explain yourself.

I dont have to explain myself to you.

Not to me. To yourself. I thought you might have something to say.

You go to hell.

You surprise me, that's all. I expected something different. It calls past events into question. Dont you think so?

You think I'd trade places with you?

Yes. I do. I'm here and you are there. In a few minutes I will still be here.

Wells looked out the darkened window. I know where the satchel is, he said.

If you knew where the satchel was you would have it.

I was going to have to wait until there was no one around. Till night. Two in the morning. Something like that.

You know where the satchel is.

Yes.

I know something better.

What's that.

I know where it's going to be.

And where is that.

It will be brought to me and placed at my feet.

Wells wiped his mouth with the back of his hand. It wouldnt cost you anything. It's twenty minutes from here.

You know that's not going to happen. Dont you?

Wells didnt answer.

Dont you?

You go to hell.

You think you can put it off with your eyes.

What do you mean?

You think that as long as you keep looking at me you can put it off.

I dont think that.

Yes you do. You should admit your situation. There would be more dignity in it. I'm trying to help you.

You son of a bitch.

You think you wont close your eyes. But you will.

Wells didnt answer. Chigurh watched him. I know what else you think, he said.

You dont know what I think.

You think I'm like you. That it's just greed. But I'm not like you. I live a simple life.

Just do it.

You wouldnt understand. A man like you.

Just do it.

Yes, Chigurh said. They always say that. But they dont mean it, do they?

You piece of shit.

It's not good, Carson. You need to compose yourself. If you dont respect me what must you think of yourself? Look at where you are.

You think you're outside of everything, Wells said. But you're not.

Not everything. No.

You're not outside of death.

It doesnt mean to me what it does to you.

You think I'm afraid to die?

Yes.

Just do it. Do it and goddamn you.

It's not the same, Chigurh said. You've been giving up things for years to get here. I dont think I even understood that. How does a man decide in what order to abandon his life? We're in the same line of work. Up to a point. Did you hold me in such contempt? Why would you do that? How did you let yourself get in this situation?

Wells looked out at the street. What time is it? he said.

Chigurh raised his wrist and looked at his watch. Eleven fifty-seven he said.

Wells nodded. By the old woman's calendar I've got three more minutes. Well the hell with it. I think I saw all this coming a long time ago. Almost like a dream. Déjà vu. He looked at Chigurh. I'm not interested in your opinions, he said. Just do it. You goddamned psychopath. Do it and goddamn you to hell.

He did close his eyes. He closed his eyes and he turned his head and he raised one hand to fend away what could not be fended away. Chigurh shot him in the face. Everything that Wells had ever known or thought or loved drained slowly down the wall behind him. His mother's face, his First Communion, women he had known. The faces of men as they died on their knees before him. The body of a child dead in a road-side ravine in another country. He lay half headless on the bed with his arms outflung, most of his right hand missing. Chigurh rose and picked up the empty casing off the rug and blew into it and put it in his pocket and looked at his watch. The new day was still a minute away.

He went down the back stairs and crossed the parking lot to Wells' car and sorted out the doorkey from the ring of keys Wells carried and opened the door and checked the car inside front and rear and under the seats. It was a rental car and there was nothing in it but the rental contract in the doorpocket. He shut the door and hobbled back and opened the trunk. Nothing. He went around to the driver side and opened the door and popped the hood and walked up front and raised the hood and looked in the engine compartment and then closed the hood and stood looking at the hotel. While he was standing there Wells' phone rang. He fished the phone from his pocket and pushed the button and put it to his ear. Yes, he said.

Moss made his way down the ward and back again holding on to the nurse's arm. She said encouraging things to him in spanish. They turned at the end of the bay and started back. The sweat stood on his forehead. Ándale, she said. Qué bueno. He nodded. Damn right bueno, he said.

Late in the night he woke from a troubling dream and struggled down the hallway and asked to use the telephone. He dialed the number in Odessa and leaned heavily on the counter and listened to it ring. It rang a long time. Finally her mother answered.

It's Llewelyn.

She dont want to talk to you.

Yes she does.

Do you know what time it is?

I dont care what time it is. Dont you hang up this phone.

I told her what was goin to happen, didnt I? Chapter and verse. I said: This is what will come to pass. And now it has come to pass.

Dont you hang up this phone. You get her and you put her on.

When she picked up the phone she said: I didnt think you'd do me thisaway.

Hello darlin, how are you? Are you all right, Llewelyn? What happened to them words?

Where are you.

Piedras Negras.

What am I supposed to do, Llewelyn?

Are you all right?

No I'm not all right. How would I be all right? People callin here about you. I had the sheriff up here from Terrell County. Showed up at the damn door. I thought you was dead.

I aint dead. What did you tell him?

What could I tell him?

He might con you into sayin somethin.

You're hurt, aint you?

What makes you say that?

I can hear it in your voice. Are you okay?

I'm okay.

Where are you?

I told you where I was.

You sound like you're in a bus station.

Carla Jean I think you need to get out of there.

Out of where?

Out of that house.

You're scarin me, Llewelyn. Out of here to go where?

It dont matter. I just dont think you should stay there. You could go to a motel.

And do what with Mama?

She'll be all right.

She'll be all right?

Yes.

You dont know that.

Llewelyn didnt answer.

Do you?

I just dont think anybody will bother her.

You dont think?

You need to get out. Just take her with you.

I cant take my mama to a motel. She's sick if you aint forgot.

What did the sheriff say.

Said he was lookin for you, what do you think he said?

What else did he say.

She didnt answer.

Carla Jean?

She sounded like she was crying.

What else did he say, Carla Jean?

He said you was fixin to get yourself killed.

Well, that's what he would say.

She was quiet a long time.

Carla Jean?

Llewelyn, I dont even want the money. I just want us to be back like we was.

We will be.

No we wont. I've thought about it. It's a false god.

Yeah. But it's real money.

She said his name again and then she did begin to cry. He tried to talk to her but she didnt answer. He stood there listening to her sobbing quietly in Odessa. What do you want me to do? he said.

She didnt answer.

Carla Jean?

I want things to be like they was.

If I tell you I'll try and fix everthing will you do what I asked you?

Yes. I will.

I've got a number here I can call. Somebody that can help us.

Can you trust them?

I dont know. I just know I cant trust nobody else. I'll call you tomorrow. I didnt think they'd find you up there or I never would of sent you. I'll call you tomorrow.

He hung up the phone and dialed the mobile number that Wells had given him. It answered on the second ring but it wasnt Wells. I think I got the wrong number, he said.

You dont have the wrong number. You need to come see me.

Who is this?

You know who it is.

Moss leaned on the counter, his forehead against his fist.

Where's Wells?

He cant help you now. What kind of a deal did you cut with him?

I didnt cut any kind of a deal.

Yes you did. How much was he going to give you?

I dont know what you're talkin about.

Where's the money.

What did you do with Wells.

We had a difference of opinion. You dont need to concern yourself about Wells. He's out of the picture. You need to talk to me.

I dont need to talk to you.

I think you do. Do you know where I'm going?

Why would I care where you're goin?

Do you know where I'm going?

Moss didnt answer.

Are you there?

I'm here.

I know where you are.

Yeah? Where am I?

You're in the hospital at Piedras Negras. But that's not where I'm going. Do you know where I'm going?

Yeah. I know where you're goin.

You can turn all this around.

Why would I believe you?

You believed Wells.

I didnt believe Wells.

You called him.

So I called him.

Tell me what you want me to do.

Moss shifted his weight. Sweat stood on his forehead. He didnt answer.

Tell me something. I'm waiting.

I could be waitin for you when you get there you know, Moss said. Charter a plane. You thought about that?

That would be okay. But you wont.

How do you know I wont?

You wouldnt have told me. Anyway, I have to go.

You know they wont be there.

It doesnt make any difference where they are.

So what are you goin up there for.

You know how this is going to turn out, dont you?

No. Do you?

Yes. I do. I think you do too. You just havent accepted it yet. So this is what I'll do. You bring me the money and I'll let her walk. Otherwise she's accountable. The same as you. I dont know if you care about that. But that's the best deal you're going to get. I wont tell you you can save yourself because you cant.

I'm goin to bring you somethin all right, Moss said. I've

decided to make you a special project of mine. You aint goin to have to look for me at all.

I'm glad to hear that. You were beginning to disappoint me.

You wont be disappointed.

Good.

You dont have to by god worry about bein disappointed.

He left before daylight dressed in the muslin hospital gown with the overcoat over it. The skirt of the overcoat was stiff with blood. He had no shoes. In the inside pocket of the coat was the money he'd folded away there, stiff and bloodstained.

He stood in the street looking toward the lights. He'd no notion where he was. The concrete cold under his feet. He made his way down to the corner. A few cars passed. He walked down to the lights at the next corner and stopped and leaned with one hand against the building. He had two white lozenges in his overcoat pocket that he'd saved and he took one now, swallowing it dry. He thought he was going to vomit. He stood there for a long time. There was a windowsill there he'd have sat on save that it was spiked with pointed iron bars to discourage loiterers. A cab went by and he raised one hand but it kept going. He was going to have to go out into the street and after a while he did. He'd been tottering there for some time when another cab passed and he raised his hand and it pulled to the curb.

The driver studied him. Moss leaned on the window. Can you take me across the bridge? he said.

To the other side.

Yes. To the other side.

You got monies.

Yes. I got monies.

The driver looked dubious. Twenty dollars, he said.

Okay.

At the gate the guard leaned down and regarded him where he sat in the dim rear of the cab. What country were you born in? he said.

The United States.

What are you bringing in?

Not anything.

The guard studied him. Would you mind stepping out here? he said.

Moss pushed down on the doorhandle and leaned on the front seat to ease himself out of the cab. He stood.

What happened to your shoes?

I dont know.

You dont have any clothes on, do you?

I got clothes on.

The second guard was waving the cars past. He pointed for the cabdriver. Would you please pull your cab over into that second space there?

The driver put the cab in gear.

Would you mind stepping away from the vehicle?

Moss stepped away. The cab pulled into the parking area and the driver cut the engine. Moss looked at the guard. The guard seemed to be waiting for him to say something but he didnt.

They took him inside and sat him in a steel chair in a small white office. Another man came in and stood leaning against a steel desk. He looked him over.

How much have you had to drink?

I aint had anything to drink.

What happened to you?

What do you mean?

What happened to your clothes.

I dont know.

Do you have any identification?

No.

Nothing.

No.

The man leaned back, his arms crossed at his chest. He said: Who do you think gets to go through this gate into the United States of America?

I dont know. American citizens.

Some American citizens. Who do you think decides that?

You do I reckon.

That's correct. And how do I decide?

I dont know.

I ask questions. If I get sensible answers then they get to go to America. If I dont get sensible answers they dont. Is there anything about that that you dont understand?

No sir.

Then maybe you'd like to start over.

All right.

We need to hear more about why you're out here with no clothes on.

I got a overcoat on.

Are you jackin with me?

No sir.

Dont jack with me. Are you in the service?

No sir. I'm a veteran.

What branch of the service.

United States Army.

Were you in Nam?

Yessir. Two tours.

What outfit.

Twelfth Infantry.

What were your dates of tour duty.

August seventh nineteen and sixty-six to September second nineteen and sixty-eight.

The man watched him for some time. Moss looked at him and looked away. He looked toward the door, the empty hall. Sitting hunched forward in the overcoat with his elbows on his knees.

Are you all right?

Yessir. I'm all right. I got a wife that'll come and get me if you all will let me go on.

Have you got any money? You got change for a phone call?

Yessir.

He heard claws scrabbling on the tiles. A guard was standing there with a German Shepherd on a lead. The man jutted his chin at the guard. Get someone to help this man. He needs to get into town. Is the taxi gone?

Yessir. It was clean.

I know. Get someone to help him.

He looked at Moss. Where are you from?

I'm from San Saba Texas.

Does your wife know where you are?

Yessir. I talked to her here just a while ago.

Did you all have a fight?

Did who have a fight?

You and your wife.

Well. Somewhat of a one I reckon. Yessir.

You need to tell her you're sorry.

Sir?

I said you need to tell her you're sorry.

Yessir. I will.

Even if you think it was her fault.

Yessir.

Go on. Get your ass out of here.

Yessir.

Sometimes you have a little problem and you dont fix it and then all of a sudden it aint a little problem anymore. You understand what I'm tellin you?

Yessir. I do.

Go on.

Yessir.

It was almost daylight and the cab was long gone. He set out up the street. A bloody serum was leaking from his wound and it was running down the inside of his leg. People paid him little mind. He turned up Adams Street and stopped at a clothing store and peered in. Lights were on at the rear. He knocked at the door and waited and knocked again. Finally a small man in a white shirt and a black tie opened the door and looked out at him. I know you aint open, Moss said, but I need some clothes real bad. The man nodded and swung open the door. Come in, he said.

They walked side by side down the aisle toward the boot section. Tony Lama, Justin, Nocona. There were some low chairs there and Moss eased himself down and sat with his hands gripping the chair arms. I need boots and some clothes, he said. I got some medical problems and I dont want to walk around no more than what I can help.

The man nodded. Yessir, he said. Of course.

Do you carry the Larry Mahans?

No sir. We dont.

That's all right. I need a pair of Wrangler jeans thirty-two by thirty-four length. A shirt size large. Some socks. And show me some Nocona boots in a ten and a half. And I need a belt.

Yessir. Did you want to look at hats?

Moss looked across the store. I think a hat would be good. You got any of them stockman's hats with the small brim? Seven and three-eights?

Yes we do. We have a three X beaver in the Resistol and a little better grade in the Stetson. A five X, I think it is.

Let me see the Stetson. That silverbelly color.

All right sir. Are white socks all right?

White socks is all I wear.

What about underwear?

Maybe a pair of jockey shorts. Thirty-two. Or medium.

Yessir. You just make yourself comfortable. Are you all right?

I'm all right.

The man nodded and turned to go.

Can I ask you somethin? Moss said.

Yessir.

Do you get a lot of people come in here with no clothes on?

No sir. I wouldnt say a lot.

He carried the pile of new clothing with him to the dressingroom and slid off the coat and hung it from the hook on the back of the door. A pale dried blood was crusted across his sallow sunken paunch. He pushed at the edges of the tape but they wouldnt stick. He eased himself down on the wooden bench and pulled on the socks and he opened the package of shorts and took them out and pulled them over his feet and up to his knees and then stood and pulled them carefully up over the dressing. He sat again and undid the shirt from its cardboard forms and endless pins.

When he came out of the dressingroom he had the coat over his arm. He walked up and down the creaking wooden aisle. The clerk stood looking down at the boots. The lizard takes longer to break in, he said.

Yeah. Hot in the summer too. These are all right. Let's try that hat. I aint been duded up like this since I got out of the army.

The sheriff sipped his coffee and set the cup back down in the same ring on the glass desktop that he'd taken it from. They're fixin to close the hotel, he said.

Bell nodded. I aint surprised.

They all quit. That feller hadnt pulled but two shifts. I blame myself. Never occurred to me that the son of a bitch would come back. I just never even imagined such a thing.

He might never of left.

I thought about that too.

The reason nobody knows what he looks like is that they dont none of em live long enough to tell it.

This is a goddamned homicidal lunatic, Ed Tom.

Yeah. I dont think he's a lunatic though.

Well what would you call him?

I dont know. When are they fixin to close it?

It's done closed, as far as that goes.

You got a key?

Yeah. I got a key. It's a crime scene.

Why dont we go over there and look around some more.

All right. We can do that.

The first thing they saw was the transponder unit sitting on a windowsill in the hallway. Bell picked it up and turned it in his hand, looking at the dial and the knobs.

That aint a goddamn bomb is it Sheriff?

No.

That's all we need.

It's a trackin device.

So whatever it was they was trackin they found.

Probably. How long has it been settin there do you reckon?

I dont know. I think I might be able to guess what they were trackin, though.

Maybe, Bell said. There's somethin about this whole deal that dont rattle right.

It aint supposed to.

We got a ex-army colonel here with most of his head gone that you had to ID off of his fingerprints. What fingers wasnt shot off. Regular army. Fourteen years service. Not a piece of paper on him.

He'd been robbed.

Yeah.

What do you know about this that you aint tellin, Sheriff?

You got the same facts I got.

I aint talkin about facts. Do you think this whole mess has moved south?

Bell shook his head. I dont know.

You got a dog in this hunt?

Not really. A couple of kids from my county that might be sort of involved that ought not to be.

Sort of involved.

Yeah.

Are we talkin kin?

No. Just people from my county. People I'm supposed to be lookin after.

He handed the transponder unit to the sheriff.

What am I supposed to do with this?

It's Maverick County property. Crime scene evidence.

The sheriff shook his head. Dope, he said.

Dope.

They sell that shit to schoolkids.

It's worse than that.

How's that?

Schoolkids buy it.

VII

I wont talk about the war neither. I was supposed to be a war hero and I lost a whole squad of men. Got decorated for it. They died and I got a medal. I dont even need to know what you think about that. There aint a day I dont remember it. Some boys I know come back they went on to school up at Austin on the GI Bill, they had hard things to say about their people. Some of em did. Called em a bunch of rednecks and all such as that. Didnt like their politics. Two generations in this country is a long time. You're talkin about the early settlers. I used to tell em that havin your wife and children killed and scalped and gutted like fish has a tendency to make some people irritable but they didnt seem to know what I was talkin about. I think the sixties in this country sobered some of em up. I hope it did. I read in the papers here a while back some teachers come across a survey that was sent out back in the thirties to a number of schools around the country. Had this questionnaire about what was the problems with teachin in the schools. And they come across these forms, they'd been filled out and sent in from around the country answerin these questions. And the biggest problems they could name was things like talkin in class and runnin in the hallways. Chewin gum. Copyin homework. Things of that nature. So they got one of them forms that was blank and printed up a bunch of em and sent em back out to the same schools. Forty years later. Well, here come the answers back. Rape, arson, murder. Drugs. Suicide. So I think about that. Because a lot of the time ever when I say anything about how the world is goin to hell in a handbasket people will just sort of smile and tell me I'm gettin old. That it's one of the symptoms. But my feelin about that is that anybody that cant tell the difference between rapin and murderin people and chewin gum has got a whole lot bigger of a problem than what I've got. Forty years is not a long time neither. Maybe the next forty of it will bring some of em out from under the ether. If it aint too late.

Here a year or two back me and Loretta went to a conference in Corpus Christi and I got set next to this woman, she was the wife of somebody or other. And she kept talkin about the right wing this and the right wing that. I aint even sure what she meant by it. The people I know are mostly just common people. Common as dirt, as the sayin goes. I told her that and she looked at me funny. She thought I was sayin somethin bad about em, but of course that's a high compliment in my part of the world. She kept on, kept on. Finally told me, said: I dont like the way this country is headed. I want my granddaughter to be able to have an abortion. And I said well mam I dont think you got any worries about the way the *country is headed. The way I see it goin I dont have much doubt but what she'll be able to have an abortion. I'm goin to say that not only will she be able to have an abortion, she'll be able to have you put to sleep. Which pretty much ended the conversation.*

Chigurh limped up the seventeen flights of concrete steps in the cool concrete well and when he got to the steel door on the landing he shot the cylinder out of the lock with the plunger of the stungun and opened the door and stepped into the hallway and shut the door behind him. He stood leaning against the door with the shotgun in both hands, listening. Breathing no harder than if he'd just got up out of a chair. He went down the hallway and picked the crushed cylinder out of the floor and put it in his pocket and went on to the elevator and stood listening again. He took off his boots and stood them by the elevator door and went down the hallway in his sockfeet, walking slowly, favoring his wounded leg.

The doors to the office were open onto the hallway. He stopped. He thought that perhaps the man did not see his own shadow on the outer hallway wall, illdefined but there. Chigurh thought it an odd oversight but he knew that fear of an enemy can often blind men to other hazards, not least the shape which they themselves make in the world. He slipped the strap from his shoulder and lowered the airtank to the floor. He studied the stance of the man's shadow framed there by the light from the smoked glass window behind him. He pushed the shotgun's follower slightly back with the heel of his hand to check the chambered round and pushed the safety off.

The man was holding a small pistol at the level of his belt. Chigurh stepped into the doorway and shot him in the throat with a load of number ten shot. The size collectors use to take bird specimens. The man fell back through his swivel-chair knocking it over and went to the floor and lay there twitching and gurgling. Chigurh picked up the smoking shotgun shell from the carpet and put it in his pocket and walked into the room with the pale smoke still drifting from the canister fitted to the end of the sawed-off barrel. He walked around behind the desk and stood looking down at the man. The man was lying on his back and he had one hand over his throat but the blood was pumping steadily through his fingers and out onto the rug. His face was full of small holes but his right eye seemed intact and he looked up at Chigurh and tried to speak from out of his bubbling mouth. Chigurh dropped to one knee and leaned on the shotgun and looked at him. What is it? he said. What are you trying to tell me?

The man moved his head. The blood gurgled in his throat.

Can you hear me? Chigurh said.

He didnt answer.

I'm the man you sent Carson Wells to kill. Is that what you wanted to know?

He watched him. He was wearing a blue nylon runningsuit and a pair of white leather shoes. Blood was starting to pool about his head and he was shivering as if he were cold.

The reason I used the birdshot was that I didnt want to break the glass. Behind you. To rain glass on people in the street. He nodded toward the window where the man's upper silhouette stood outlined in the small gray pockmarks the lead had left in the glass. He looked at the man. The man's hand had gone slack at his throat and the blood had slowed. He looked at the pistol lying there. He rose and pushed the safety back on the shotgun and stepped past the man to the window and inspected the pockings the lead had made. When he looked down at the man again the man was dead. He crossed the room and stood at the doorway listening. He went out and down the hall and collected his tank and the stungun and got his boots and stepped into them and pulled them up. Then he walked down the corridor and went out through the metal door and down the concrete steps to the garage where he'd left his vehicle.

When they got to the bus station it was just breaking daylight, gray and cold and a light rain falling. She leaned forward over the seat and paid the driver and gave him a two dollar tip. He got out and went around to the trunk and opened it and got their bags and set them in the portico and brought the walker around to her mother's side and opened the door. Her mother turned and began to struggle out into the rain.

Mama will you wait? I need to get around there.

I knowed this is what it would come to, the mother said. I said it three year ago.

It aint been three years.

I used them very words.

Just wait till I get around there.

In the rain, her mother said. She looked up at the cabdriver. I got cancer, she said. Now look at this. Not even a home to go to.

Yes mam.

We're goin to El Paso Texas. You know how many people I know in El Paso Texas?

No mam.

She paused with her arm on the door and held up her hand and made an O with her thumb and forefinger. That's how many, she said.

Yes mam.

They sat in the coffeeshop surrounded by their bags and parcels and stared out at the rain and at the idling buses. At the gray day breaking. She looked at her mother. Did you want some more coffee? she said.

The old woman didnt answer.

You aint speakin, I reckon.

I dont know what there is to speak about.

Well I dont guess I do either.

Whatever you all done you done. I dont know why I ought to have to run from the law.

We aint runnin from the law, Mama.

You couldnt call on em to help you though, could you?

Call on who?

The law.

No. We couldnt.

That's what I thought.

The old woman adjusted her teeth with her thumb and stared out the window. After a while the bus came. The driver stowed her walker in the luggage bay under the bus and they helped her up the steps and put her in the first seat. I got cancer, she told the driver.

Carla Jean put their bags in the bin overhead and sat down. The old woman didnt look at her. Three years ago, she said. You didnt have to have no dream about it. No revelation nor nothin. I dont give myself no credit. Anybody could of told you the same thing.

Well I wasnt askin.

The old woman shook her head. Looking out through the window and down at the table they'd vacated. I give myself no credit, she said. I'd be the last in the world to do that.

Chigurh pulled up across the street and shut off the engine. He turned off the lights and sat watching the darkened house. The green diode numerals on the radio put the time at 1:17.

He sat there till 1:22 and then he took the flashlight from the glovebox and got out and closed the truck door and crossed the street to the house.

He opened the screen door and punched out the cylinder and walked in and shut the door behind him and stood listening. There was a light coming from the kitchen and he walked down the hallway with the flashlight in one hand and the shotgun in the other. When he got to the doorway he stopped and listened again. The light came from a bare bulb on the back porch. He went on into the kitchen.

A bare formica and chrome table in the center of the room with a box of cereal standing on it. The shadow of the kitchen window lying on the linoleum floor. He crossed the room and opened the refrigerator and looked in. He put the shotgun in the crook of his arm and took out a can of orange soda and opened it with his forefinger and stood drinking it, listening for anything that might follow the metallic click of the can. He drank and set the half-empty can on the counter and shut the refrigerator door and walked through the diningroom and into the livingroom and sat in an easy chair in the corner and looked out at the street.

After a while he rose and crossed the room and went up the stairs. He stood listening at the head of the stairwell. When he entered the old woman's room he could smell the sweet musty odor of sickness and he thought for a moment she might even be lying there in the bed. He switched on the flashlight and went into the bathroom. He stood reading the labels of the pharmacy bottles on the vanity. He looked out the window at the street below, the dull winter light from the streetlamps. Two in the morning. Dry. Cold. Silent. He went out and down the hallway to the small bedroom at the rear of the house.

He emptied her bureau drawers out onto the bed and sat sorting through her things, holding up from time to time some item and studying it in the bluish light from the yardlamp. A plastic hairbrush. A cheap fairground bracelet. Weighing these things in his hand like a medium who might thereby divine some fact concerning the owner. He sat turning the pages in a photo album. School friends. Family. A dog. A house not this one. A man who may have been her father. He put two pictures of her in his shirtpocket.

There was a ceiling fan overhead. He got up and pulled the chain and lay down on the bed with the shotgun alongside him, watching the wooden blades wheel slowly in the light from the window. After a while he got up and took the chair from the desk in the corner and tilted it and pushed the top backladder up under the doorknob. Then he sat on the bed and pulled off his boots and stretched out and went to sleep.

In the morning he walked through the house again upstairs and down and then returned to the bathroom at the end of the hall to shower. He left the curtain pulled back, the water spraying onto the floor. The hallway door open and the shotgun lying on the vanity a foot away.

He dried the dressing on his leg with a hairdryer and

shaved and dressed and went down to the kitchen and ate a bowl of cereal and milk, walking through the house as he ate. In the livingroom he stopped and looked at the mail lying in the floor beneath the brass slot in the front door. He stood there, chewing slowly. Then he set bowl and spoon on the coffeetable and crossed the room and bent over and picked up the mail and stood sorting through it. He sat in a chair by the door and opened the phone bill and cupped the envelope and blew into it.

He glanced down the list of calls. Halfway down was the Terrell County Sheriff's Department. He folded the bill and put it back in the envelope and put the envelope in his shirt-pocket. Then he looked through the other pieces of mail again. He rose and went into the kitchen and got the shotgun off the table and came back and stood where he'd stood before. He crossed to a cheap mahogany desk and opened the top drawer. The drawer was stuffed with mail. He laid the shotgun down and sat in the chair and pulled the mail out and piled it on the desk and began to go through it.

Moss spent the day in a cheap motel on the edge of town sleeping naked in the bed with his new clothes on wire hangers in the closet. When he woke the shadows were long in the motel courtyard and he struggled up and sat on the edge of the bed. A pale bloodstain the size of his hand on the sheets. There was a paper bag on the night table that held things he'd bought from a drugstore in town and he picked it up and limped into the bathroom. He showered and shaved and brushed his teeth for the first time in five days and then sat on the edge of the tub and taped fresh gauze over his wounds. Then he got dressed and called a cab.

He was standing in front of the motel office when the cab pulled up. He climbed into the rear seat, got his breath, then reached and shut the door. He regarded the face of the driver in the rearview mirror. Do you want to make some money? he said.

Yeah. I want to make some money.

Moss took five of the hundreds and tore them in two and passed one half across the back of the seat to the driver. The driver counted the torn bills and put them in his shirtpocket and looked at Moss in the mirror and waited.

What's your name?

Paul, said the driver.

You got the right attitude, Paul. I wont get you in trouble. I just dont want you to leave me somewheres that I dont want to be left.

All right.

Have you got a flashlight?

Yeah. I got a flashlight.

Let me have it.

The driver passed the flashlight to the back.

You're the man, Moss said.

Where are we going.

Down the river road.

I aint pickin nobody up.

We're not pickin anybody up.

The driver watched him in the mirror. No drogas, he said.

No drogas.

The driver waited.

I'm goin to pick up a briefcase. It belongs to me. You can look inside if you want. Nothin illegal.

I can look inside.

Yes you can.

I hope you're not jerkin me around.

No.

I like money but I like stayin out of jail even better.

I'm the same way myself, Moss said.

They drove slowly up the road toward the bridge. Moss leaned forward over the seat. I want you to park under the bridge, he said.

All right.

I'm goin to unscrew the bulb out of this domelight.

They watch this road round the clock, the driver said.

I know that.

The driver pulled off of the road and shut off the engine and the lights and looked at Moss in the mirror. Moss took the bulb from the light and laid it in the plastic lens and handed it across the seat to the driver and opened the door. I should be back in just a few minutes, he said.

The cane was dusty, the stalks close grown. He pushed his

way through carefully, holding the light at his knees with his hand partly across the lens.

The case was sitting in the brake rightside up and intact as if someone had simply set it there. He switched off the light and picked it up and made his way back in the dark, taking his sight by the span of the bridge overhead. When he got to the cab he opened the door and set the case in the seat and got in carefully and shut the door. He handed the flashlight to the driver and leaned back in the seat. Let's go, he said.

What's in there, the driver said.

Money.

Money?

Money.

The driver started the engine and pulled out onto the road.

Turn the lights on, Moss said.

He turned the lights on.

How much money?

A lot of money. What will you take to drive me to San Antonio.

The driver thought about it. You mean on top of the five hundred.

Yes.

How about a grand all in.

Everthing.

Yes.

You got it.

The driver nodded. Then how about the other half of these five caesars I already got.

Moss took the bills from his pocket and handed them across the back of the seat.

What if the Migra stop us.

They wont stop us, Moss said.

How do you know?

There's too much shit still down the road that I got to deal with. It aint goin to end here.

I hope you're right.

Trust me, Moss said.

I hate hearin them words, the driver said. I always did.

Have you ever said them?

Yeah. I've said em. That's how come I know what they're worth.

He spent the night in a Rodeway Inn on highway 90 just west of town and in the morning he went down and got a paper and climbed laboriously back to his room. He couldnt buy a gun from a dealer because he had no identification but he could buy one out of the paper and he did. A Tec-9 with two extra magazines and a box and a half of shells. The man delivered the gun to his door and he paid him in cash. He turned the piece in his hand. It had a greenish parkerized finish. Semiautomatic. When was the last time you fired it? he said.

I aint never fired it.

Are you sure it fires?

Why would it not?

I dont know.

Well I dont either.

After he left Moss walked out onto the prairie behind the motel with one of the motel pillows under his arm and he wrapped the pillow about the muzzle of the gun and fired off three rounds and then stood there in the cold sunlight watching the feathers drift across the gray chaparral, thinking about his life, what was past and what was to come. Then he turned and walked slowly back to the motel leaving the burnt pillow on the ground.

He rested in the lobby and then climbed up to the room again. He bathed in the tub and looked at the exit hole in his lower back in the bathroom mirror. It looked pretty ugly. There were drains in both holes that he wanted to pull out but he didnt. He pulled loose the plaster on his arm and looked at the deep furrow the bullet had cut there and then taped the dressing back again. He dressed and put some more of the bills into the back pocket of his jeans and he fitted the pistol and the magazines into the case and closed it and called a cab and picked up the document case and went out and down the stairs.

He bought a 1978 Ford pickup with four wheel drive and a 460 engine from a lot on North Broadway and paid the man in cash and got the title notarized in the office and put the title in the glovebox and drove away. He drove back to the motel and checked out and left, the Tec-9 under the seat and the document case and his bag of clothes sitting in the floor on the passenger side of the truck.

At the onramp at Boerne there was a girl hitchhiking and Moss pulled over and blew the horn and watched her in the rearview mirror. Running, her blue nylon knapsack slung over one shoulder. She climbed in the truck and looked at him. Fifteen, sixteen. Red hair. How far are you goin? she said.

Can you drive?

Yeah. I can drive. It aint no stick shift is it?

No. Get out and come around.

She left her knapsack on the seat and got out of the truck and crossed in front of it. Moss pushed the knapsack into the floor and eased himself across and she got in and put the truck in drive and they pulled out onto the interstate.

How old are you?

Eighteen.

Bullshit. What are you doin out here? Dont you know it's dangerous to hitchhike?

Yeah. I know it.

He took off his hat and put it on the seat beside him and leaned back and closed his eyes. Dont go over the speed limit, he said. You get us stopped by the cops and you and me both will be in a shitpot full of trouble.

All right.

I'm serious. You go over the speed limit and I'll set your ass out by the side of the road.

All right.

He tried to sleep but he couldnt. He was in a lot of pain. After a while he sat up and got his hat off the seat and put it on and looked over at the speedometer.

Can I ask you somethin? she said.

You can ask.

Are you runnin from the law?

Moss eased himself in the seat and looked at her and looked out at the highway. What makes you ask that?

On account of what you said back yonder. About bein stopped by the police.

What if I was?

Then I think I ought to just get out up here.

You dont think that. You just want to know where you stand.

She looked at him out of the corner of her eye. Moss studied the passing country. If you spent three days with me, he said, I could have you holdin up gas stations. Be no trick at all.

She gave him a funny little half smile. Is that what you do? she said. Hold up gas stations?

No. I dont have to. Are you hungry?

I'm all right.

When did you eat last.

I dont like for people to start askin me when I eat last.

All right. When did you eat last?

I knowed you was a smart-ass from the time I got in the truck.

Yeah. Pull off up here at this next exit. It's supposed to be four miles. And reach me that machinegun from under the seat.

Bell drove slowly across the cattleguard and got out and closed the gate and got back in the truck and drove across the pasture and parked at the well and got out and walked over to the tank. He put his hand in the water and raised a palmful and let it spill again. He took off his hat and passed his wet hand through his hair and looked up at the windmill. He looked out at the slow dark elliptic of the blades turning in the dry and windbent grass. A low wooden trundling under his feet. Then he just stood there paying the brim of his hat slowly through his fingers. The posture of a man perhaps who has just buried something. I dont know a damn thing, he said.

When he got home she had supper waiting. He dropped the keys to the pickup in the kitchen drawer and went to the sink to wash his hands. His wife laid a piece of paper on the counter and he stood looking at it.

Did she say where she was? This is a West Texas number.

She just said it was Carla Jean and give the number.

He went to the sideboard and called. She and her grandmother were in a motel outside of El Paso. I need for you to tell me somethin, she said.

All right.

Is your word good?

Yes it is.

Even to me?

I'd say especially to you.

He could hear her breathing in the receiver. Traffic in the distance.

Sheriff?

Yes mam.

If I tell you where he called from do you give your word that no harm will come to him.

I can give my word that no harm will come to him from me. I can do that.

After a while she said: Okay.

The man sitting at the little plywood table that folded up from the wall onto a hinged leg finished writing on the pad of paper and took off the headset and laid it on the table in front of him and passed both hands backwards over the sides of his black hair. He turned and looked toward the rear of the trailer where the second man was stretched out on the bed. Listo? he said.

The man sat up and swung his legs to the floor. He sat there for a minute and then he rose and came forward.

You got it?

I got it.

He tore the sheet off the pad and handed it to him and he read it and folded it and put it into his shirtpocket. Then he reached up and opened one of the kitchen cabinets and took out a camouflage-finished submachinegun and a pair of spare clips and pushed open the door and stepped down into the lot and shut the door behind him. He crossed the gravel to where a black Plymouth Barracuda was parked and opened the door and pitched the machinegun in on the far seat and lowered himself in and shut the door and started the engine. He blipped the throttle a couple of times and then pulled out onto the blacktop and turned on the lights and shifted into second gear and went up the road with the car squatting on the big rear tires and fishtailing and the tires whining and unspooling clouds of rubbersmoke behind him.

VIII

I've lost a lot of friends over these last few years. Not all of em older than me neither. One of the things you realize about gettin older is that not everbody is goin to get older with you. You try to help the people that're payin your salary and of course you cant help but think about the kind of record you leave. This county has not had a unsolved homicide in forty-one years. Now we got nine of em in one week. Will they be solved? I dont know. Ever day is against you. Time is not on your side. I dont know as it'd be any compliment if you was known for second guessin a bunch of dopedealers. Not that they have all that much trouble second guessin us. They dont have no respect for the law? That aint half of it. They dont even think about the law. It dont seem to even concern em. Of course here a while back in San Antonio they shot and killed a federal judge. I guess he concerned em. Add to that that there's peace officers along this border gettin rich off of narcotics. That's a painful thing to know. Or it is for me. I dont believe that was true even ten years ago. A crooked peace officer is just a damned abomination. That's all you can say about it. He's ten times worse than the criminal. And this aint goin away. And that's about the only thing I do know. It aint goin away. Where would it go to?

And this may sound ignorant but I think for me the worst of it is knowin that probably the only reason I'm even still alive is that they have no respect for me. And that's very painful. Very painful. It has done got way beyond anything you might of thought about even a few years ago. Here a while back they found a DC-4 over in Presidio County. Just settin out in the desert. They had come in there of a night and graded out a sort of landin strip and set out rows of tarbarrels for lights but there was no way you could of flown that thing back out of there. It was stripped out to the walls. Just had a pilot's seat in it. You could smell the marijuana, you didnt need no dog. Well the sheriff over there—and I wont say his name—he wanted to get set up and nail em when they come back for the plane and finally somebody told him that they wasnt nobody comin back. Never had been. When he finally understood what it was they was tellin him he just got real quiet and then he turned around and got in his car and left.

When they was havin them dope wars down across the border you could not buy a half quart masonjar nowheres. To put up your preserves and such. Your chow chow. They wasnt none to be had. What it was they was usin them jars to put handgrenades in. If you flew over somebody's house or compound and you dropped grenades on em they'd go off fore they hit the ground. So what they done was they'd pull the pin and stick em down in the jar and screw the lid back on. Then whenever they hit the ground the glass'd break and release the spoon. The lever. They would preload cases of them things. Hard to believe that a man would ride around at night in a small plane with a cargo such as that, but they done it.

I think if you were Satan and you were settin around tryin to think up somethin that would just bring the human race to its knees what you would probably come up with is narcotics. Maybe he did. I told that to somebody at breakfast the other mornin and they asked me if I believed in Satan. I said Well that aint the point. And they said I know but do you? I had to think about that. I guess as a boy I did. Come the middle years my belief I reckon had waned somewhat. Now I'm startin to lean back the other way. He explains a lot of things that otherwise dont have no explanation. Or not to me they dont.

Moss set the case in the booth and eased himself in after it. He lifted the menu from the wire rack where it stood along with the mustard and ketchup. She scooted into the booth opposite. He didnt look up. What are you havin, he said.

I dont know. I aint looked at the menu.

He spun the menu around and slid it in front of her and turned and looked for the waitress.

What are you? the girl said.

What am I havin?

No. What are you. Are you a character?

He studied her. The only people I know that know what a character is, he said, is other characters.

I might just be a fellow traveler.

Fellow traveler.

Yeah.

Well you are now.

You're hurt, aint you?

What makes you say that?

You cant hardly walk.

Maybe it's just a old war injury.

I dont think so. What happened to you?

You mean lately?

Yeah. Lately.

You dont need to know.

Why not?

I dont want you gettin all excited on me.

What makes you think I'd get excited?

Cause bad girls like bad boys. What are you goin to have?

I dont know. What is it you do?

Three weeks ago I was a law abidin citizen. Workin a nine to five job. Eight to four, anyways. Things happen to you they happen. They dont ask first. They dont require your permission.

That's the truth if I ever heard it told, she said.

You hang around me you'll hear some more of it.

You think I'm a bad girl?

I think you'd like to be.

What's in that briefcase?

Briefs.

What's in it.

I could tell you, but then I'd have to kill you.

You aint supposed to carry a gun in a public place. Did you not know that? In particular a gun such as that.

Let me ask you somethin.

Go ahead.

When the shootin starts would you rather be armed or be legal?

I dont want to be around no shootin.

Yes you do. It's wrote all over you. You just dont want to get shot. What are you havin?

What are you?

Cheeseburger and a chocolate milk.

The waitress came and they ordered. She got the hot beef sandwich with mashed potatoes and gravy. You aint even asked me where I was goin, she said.

I know where you're goin.

Where am I goin then.

Down the road.

That aint no answer.

It's more than just a answer.

You dont know everthing.

No I dont.

You ever kill anybody?

Yeah, he said. You?

She looked embarrassed. You know I aint never killed nobody.

I dont know that.

Well I aint.

You aint, then.

You aint done, either. Are you?

Done what.

What I just said.

Killin people?

She looked around to see if they might be overheard.

Yes, she said.

Be hard to say.

After a while the waitress brought their plates. He bit the corner off a packet of mayonnaise and squeezed out the contents over his cheeseburger and reached for the ketchup. Where you from? he said.

She took a drink of her iced tea and wiped her mouth with the paper napkin. Port Arthur, she said.

He nodded. He took up the cheeseburger in both hands and bit into it and sat back, chewing. I aint never been to Port Arthur.

I aint never seen you there.

How could you of seen me there if I aint never been there?

I couldnt. I was just sayin I aint. I was agreein with you.

Moss shook his head.

They ate. He watched her.

I reckon you're on your way to California.

How did you know that?

That's the direction you're headed in.

Well that's where I'm goin.

You got any money?

What's it to you?

It aint nothin to me. Do you?

I got some.

He finished the cheeseburger and wiped his hands on the paper napkin and drank the rest of the milk. Then he reached in his pocket and took out the roll of hundreds and unfolded them. He counted out a thousand dollars onto the formica and pushed it toward her and put the roll back in his pocket. Let's go, he said.

What's that for?

To go to California on.

What do I gotta do for it?

You dont have to do nothin. Even a blind sow finds a acorn ever once in a while. Put that up and let's go.

They paid and walked out to the truck. You wasnt callin me a sow back yonder was you?

Moss ignored her. Give me the keys, he said.

She took the keys from her pocket and handed them over. I thought maybe you'd forgot I had em, she said.

I dont forget much.

I could of just slipped off like I was goin to the ladies room and took your truck and left you settin there.

No you couldnt of.

Why not?

Get in the truck.

They got in and he set the case between them and pulled the Tec-9 out of his belt and slid it under the seat.

Why not? she said.

Dont be ignorant all your life. In the first place I could see all the way to the front door and out the parkin lot clear to the truck. In the second place even if I was dumb-ass enough to set with my back to the door I'd of just called a cab and run you down and pulled you over and beat the shit out of you and left you layin there.

She got real quiet. He put the key in the ignition and started the truck and backed it out.

Would you of done that?

What do you think?

When they pulled into Van Horn it was seven oclock at night. She'd slept a good part of the way, curled up with her knapsack for a pillow. He pulled into a truckstop and shut off the engine and her eyes snapped open like a deer's. She sat up and looked at him and then looked out at the parking lot. Where are we? she said.

Van Horn. You hungry?

I could eat a bite.

You want some diesel fried chicken?

What?

He pointed to the sign overhead.

I aint eatin nothin like that, she said.

She was in the ladies room a long time. When she came out she wanted to know if he'd ordered.

I did. I ordered some of that chicken for you.

You aint done it, she said.

They ordered steaks. Do you live like this all the time? she said.

Sure. When you're a big time desperado the sky's the limit.

What's that on that chain?

This?

Yeah.

It's a tush off of a wild boar.

What do you wear that for?

It aint mine. I'm just keepin it for somebody.

A lady somebody?

No, a dead somebody.

The steaks came. He watched her eat. Does they anybody know where you're at? he said.

What?

I said does anybody know where you're at.

Like who?

Like anybody.

You.

I dont know where you're at because I dont know who you are.

Well that makes two of us.

You dont know who you are?

No, silly. I dont know who you are.

Well, we'll just keep it that way and they wont neither of us be out nothin. All right?

All right. What'd you ask me that for?

Moss mopped up steak gravy with a half a roll. I just thought it was probably true. For you it's a luxury. For me it's a necessity.

Why? Because they's somebody after you?

Maybe.

I do like it that way, she said. You got that part right.

It dont take long to get a taste for it, does it?

No, she said. It dont.

Well, it aint as simple as it sounds. You'll see.

Why is that.

There's always somebody knows where you're at. Knows where and why. For the most part.

Are you talkin about God?

No. I'm talkin about you.

She ate. Well, she said. You'd be in a fix if you didnt know where you was at.

I dont know. Would you?

I dont know.

Suppose you was someplace that you didnt know where it was. The real thing you wouldnt know was where someplace else was. Or how far it was. It wouldnt change nothin about where you was at.

She thought about that. I try not to think about stuff like that, she said.

You think when you get to California you'll kind of start over.

Them's my intentions.

I think maybe that's the point. There's a road goin to California and there's one comin back. But the best way would be just to show up there.

Show up there.

Yeah.

You mean and not know how you got there?

Yeah. And not know how you got there.

I dont know how you'd do that.

I dont either. That's the point.

She ate. She looked around. Can I get some coffee? she said.

You can get anything you want. You got money.

She looked at him. I guess I aint sure what the point is, she said.

The point is there aint no point.

No. I mean what you said. About knowin where you are.

He looked at her. After a while he said: It's not about knowin where you are. It's about thinkin you got there without takin anything with you. Your notions about startin over. Or anybody's. You dont start over. That's what it's about. Ever step you take is forever. You cant make it go away. None of it. You understand what I'm sayin?

I think so.

I know you dont but let me try it one more time. You think when you wake up in the mornin yesterday dont count. But yesterday is all that does count. What else is there? Your life is made out of the days it's made out of. Nothin else. You might think you could run away and change your name and I dont know what all. Start over. And then one mornin you wake up and look at the ceilin and guess who's layin there?

She nodded.

You understand what I'm sayin?

I understand that. I been there.

Yeah, I know you have.

So are you sorry you become a outlaw?

Sorry I didnt start sooner. Are you ready?

When he came out of the motel office he handed her a key.

What's that?

That's your key.

She hefted it in her hand and looked at him. Well, she said. It's up to you.

Yes it is.

I guess you're afraid I'll see what's in that bag.

Not really.

He started the truck and pulled down the parking lot behind the motel office.

Are you queer? she said.

Me? Yeah, I'm queer as a coot.

You dont look it.

Is that right? You know a lot of queers?

You dont act it I guess I should say.

Well darlin what would you know about it?

I dont know.

Say it again.

What?

Say it again. I dont know.

I dont know.

That's good. You need to practice that. It sounds good on you.

Later he went out and drove down to the quickstop. When he pulled back into the motel he sat there studying the cars in the lot. Then he got out.

He walked down to her room and tapped at the door. He waited. He tapped again. He saw the curtain move and then she opened the door. She stood there in the same jeans and T-shirt. She looked like she'd just woken up.

I know you aint old enough to drink but I thought I'd see if you wanted a beer.

Yeah, she said. I'd drink a beer.

He lifted one of the cold bottles out of the brown paper bag and handed it to her. Here you go, he said.

He'd already turned to go. She stepped out and let the door shut behind her. You dont need to rush off thataway, she said.

He stopped on the lower step.

You got another one of these in that sack?

Yeah. I got two more. And I aim to drink both of em.

I just meant maybe you could set here and drink one of em with me.

He squinted at her. You ever notice how women have trouble takin no for a answer? I think it starts about age three.

What about men?

They get used to it. They better.

I wont say a word. I'll just set here.

You wont say a word.

No.

Well that's already a lie.

Well I wont say hardly nothin. I'll be real quiet.

He sat on the step and pulled one of the beers from the bag and twisted off the cap and tilted the bottle and drank. She sat on the next step up and did the same.

You sleep a lot? he said.

I sleep when I get the chance. Yeah. You?

I aint had a night's sleep in about two weeks. I dont know what it would feel like. I think it's beginnin to make me stupid.

You dont look stupid to me.

Well, that's by your lights.

What does that mean?

Nothin. I'm just raggin you. I'll quit.

You aint got drugs in that satchel have you?

No. Why? You use drugs?

I'd smoke some weed if you had some.

Well I aint.

That's all right.

Moss shook his head. He drank.

I just meant it's all right we could just set out here and drink a beer.

Well I'm glad to hear that's all right.

Where are you headin? You aint never said.

Hard to say.

You aint goin to California though, are you?

No. I aint.

I didnt think so.

I'm goin to El Paso.

I thought you didnt know where you was goin.

Maybe I just decided.

I dont think so.

Moss didnt answer.

This is nice settin out here, she said.

I guess it depends on where you been settin.

You aint just got out of the penitentiary or somethin have you?

I just got off of death row. They'd done shaved my head for the electric chair. You can see where it's started to grow back.

You're full of it.

Be funny if it turned out to be true though, wouldnt it?

Is the law huntin you?

Everbody's huntin me.

What did you do?

I been pickin up young girls hitchhikin and buryin em out in the desert.

That aint funny.

You're right. It aint. I was just pullin your leg.

You said you'd quit.

I will.

Do you ever tell the truth?

Yeah. I tell the truth.

You're married, aint you?

Yeah.

What's your wife's name?

Carla Jean.

Is she in El Paso?

Yeah.

Does she know what you do for a livin?

Yeah. She knows. I'm a welder.

She watched him. To see what else he would say. He didnt say anything.

You aint no welder, she said.

Why aint I?

What have you got that machinegun for?

Cause they's some bad people after me.

What did you do to em?

I took somethin that belongs to em and they want it back.

That dont sound like weldin to me.

It dont, does it? I guess I hadnt thought of that.

He sipped the beer. Holding it by the neck between his thumb and forefinger.

And that's what's in that bag. Aint it?

Hard to say.

Are you a safecracker?

A safecracker?

Yeah.

Whatever give you that notion?

I dont know. Are you?

No.

Well you're somethin. Aint you?

Everbody's somethin.

You ever been to California?

Yeah. I been to California. I got a brother lives there.

Does he like it?

I dont know. He lives there.

You wouldnt live there though, would you?

No.

You think that's where I ought to go?

He looked at her and looked away again. He stretched his legs out on the concrete and crossed his boots and looked out across the parking lot toward the highway and the lights on the highway. Darlin, he said, how in the hell would I know where you ought to go?

Yeah. Well, I appreciate you givin me that money.

You're welcome.

You didnt have to do that.

I thought you wasnt goin to talk.

All right. That's a lot of money though.

It aint half what you think it is. You'll see.

I wont blow it in. I need money to get me a place to stay.

You'll be all right.

I hope so.

Best way to live in California is to be from somewheres else. Probably the best way is to be from Mars.

I hope not. Cause I aint.

You'll be all right.

Can I ask you somethin?

Yeah. Go ahead.

How old are you?

Thirty-six.

That's pretty old. I didnt know you was that old.

I know. It kind of took me by surprise my own self.

I got a feelin I ought to be afraid of you but I aint.

Well. I cant advise you on that neither. Most people'll run from their own mother to get to hug death by the neck. They cant wait to see him.

I guess that's what you think I'm doin.

I dont even want to know what you're doin.

I wonder where I'd be right now if I hadnt of met you this mornin.

I dont know.

I was always lucky. About stuff like that. About meetin people.

Well, I wouldnt speak too soon.

Why? You fixin to bury me out in the desert?

No. But there's a lot of bad luck out there. You hang around long enough and you'll come in for your share of it.

I think I done have. I believe I'm due for a change. I might even be overdue.

Yeah? Well you aint.

Why do you say that?

He looked at her. Let me tell you somethin, little sister. If there is one thing on this planet that you dont look like it's a bunch of good luck walkin around.

That's a hateful thing to say.

No it aint. I just want you to be careful. We get to El Paso I'm goin to drop you at the bus station. You got money. You dont need to be out here hitchhikin.

All right.

All right.

Would you of done what you said back yonder? About if I had of took your truck?

What's that?

You know. About beatin the crap out of me.

No.

I didn't think so.

You want to split this last beer?

All right.

Run in there and get a cup. I'll be back in a minute.

All right. You aint changed your mind have you?

About what?

You know about what.

I dont change my mind. I like to get it right the first time.

He rose and started up the walkway. She stood at the door. I'll tell you somethin I heard in a movie one time, she said.

He stopped and turned. What's that?

There's a lot of good salesmen around and you might buy somethin yet.

Well darlin you're just a little late. Cause I done bought. And I think I'll stick with what I got.

He went on up the walkway and climbed the stairs and went in.

The Barracuda pulled into a truckstop outside of Balmorhea and drove into the bay of the adjoining carwash. The driver got out and shut the door and looked at it. There was blood and other matter streaked over the glass and over the sheetmetal and he walked out and got quarters from a changemachine and came back and put them in the slot and took down the wand from the rack and washed the car and rinsed it off and got back in and pulled out onto the highway going west.

Bell left the house at seven-thirty and took 285 north to Fort Stockton. It was about a two hundred mile run to Van Horn and he reckoned he could make it in under three hours. He turned the rooflights on. About ten miles west of Fort Stockton on the I-10 interstate he passed a car burning by the side of the highway. There were police cars at the scene and one lane of the highway was blocked off. He didnt stop but it gave him an uneasy feeling. He stopped at Balmorhea and refilled his coffeebottle and he pulled into Van Horn at ten twenty-five.

He didnt know what he was looking for but he didnt have to. In the parking lot of a motel there were two Culberson County patrol cars and a state police car all with their lights going. The motel was cordoned off with yellow tape. He pulled in and parked and left his own lights on.

The deputy didnt know him but the sheriff did. They were questioning a man sitting in his shirtsleeves in the open back door of one of the cruisers. Damn if bad news dont travel fast, the sheriff said. What are you doin up here, Sheriff?

What's happened, Marvin?

Had a little shoot-out. You know anything about this?

I dont know. You got any victims?

They left out of here about a half hour ago in the ambulance. Two men and a woman. The woman was dead and the one boy I dont think is goin to make it either. The other one might.

Do you know who they were?

No. One of the men was Mexican and we're waitin for a registration on his car settin over yonder. Wasnt a one of em had any identification. On em or in the room either one.

What does this man say?

He says the Mexican started it. Says he drug the woman out of her room and the other man come out with a gun but when he seen the Mexican had a gun pointed at the woman's head he laid his own piece down. And whenever he done that the Mexican shoved the woman away and shot her and then turned and shot him. He was standin in front of 117, right yonder. Shot em with a goddamned machinegun. Accordin to this witness the old boy fell down the steps and then he picked up his gun again and shot the Mexican. Which I dont see how he done it. He was shot all to pieces. You can see the blood on the walkway yonder. We had a real good response time. About seven minutes, I think. The girl was just shot dead.

No ID.

No ID. The other old boy's truck is got dealer tags on it.

Bell nodded. He looked at the witness. The witness had asked for a cigarette and he lit it and sat smoking. He looked pretty comfortable. He looked as if he'd sat in the back of police cruisers before.

That woman, Bell said. Was she anglo?

Yeah. She was anglo. Had blonde hair. Sort of reddish, maybe.

Did you all find any dope?

Not yet. We're still lookin.

Any money?

We aint found nothin yet. The girl was checked into 121. Had a knapsack with some clothes in it and stuff was all.

Bell looked down the row of motel doors. People standing around in small groups talking. He looked at the black Barracuda.

Has that thing got anything to turn them tires with?

I'd say it would turn em pretty good. It's got a four-forty under the hood with a blower on it.

A blower?

Yep.

I dont see one.

It's one of them sidewinders. It's all under the hood.

Bell stood looking at the car. Then he turned and looked at the sheriff. Can you get away from here for a minute?

I can. What did you have in mind?

I just thought I might get you to ride over to the clinic with me.

All right. Just ride with me.

That'll be fine. Let me just park my cruiser a little better.

Hell, it's all right, Ed Tom.

Let me just pull it up here out of the way. You dont always know how quick you'll be back when you set off someplace.

At the desk the sheriff spoke to the night nurse by name. She looked at Bell.

He's up here to make a identification, the sheriff said.

She nodded and rose and put her pencil in the pages of the book she was reading. Two of em were DOA, she said. They flew that Mexican out of here in a helicopter about twenty minutes ago. Or maybe you already knew that.

Nobody tells me nothin, darlin, the sheriff said.

They followed her down the hallway. There was a thin trail of blood along the concrete floor. They wouldnt of been hard to find, would they? Bell said.

There was a red sign at the end of the hall that read Exit. Before they got there she turned and fitted a key to a steel door on the left and opened it and switched on the light. The room was raw concrete block, windowless and empty save for three steel machinist's tables on wheels. On two of them lay bodies covered with plastic sheets. She stood with her back to the open door while they filed past.

He aint a friend of yours is he Ed Tom?

No.

He took a couple of rounds in the face so I dont think he's goin to look too good. Not that I aint seen worse. That highway out there is a goddamn warzone, you tell the truth about it.

He pulled back the sheet. Bell walked around the end of the table. There was no chock under Moss's neck and his head was turned to the side. One eye partly opened. He looked like a badman on a slab. They'd sponged the blood off of him but there were holes in his face and his teeth were shot out.

Is that him?

Yeah, that's him.

You look like you wished it wasnt.

I get to tell his wife.

I'm sorry about that.

Bell nodded.

Well, the sheriff said. There aint nothin you could of done about it.

No, Bell said. But you always like to think there is.

The sheriff covered Moss's face and reached and lifted

back the plastic at the other table and looked at Bell. Bell shook his head.

They'd rented two rooms. Or he did. Paid cash. You couldnt read the name on the register. Just a scrawl.

His name was Moss.

All right. We'll get your information down at the office. Kind of a skankylookin little old girl.

Yeah.

He covered her face again. I dont reckon his wife is goin to like that part of it neither, he said.

No, I dont expect she will.

The sheriff looked at the nurse. She was still standing leaning against the door. How many times was she hit? he said. Do you know?

No I dont, Sheriff. You can look at her if you want. I dont mind and I know she wont.

That's all right. It'll be on the autopsy. Are you ready, Ed Tom?

Yeah. I was ready fore I come in here.

He sat in the sheriff's office alone with the door shut and stared at the phone on the desk. Finally he got up and went out. The deputy looked up.

He's gone home, I reckon.

Yessir, the deputy said. Can I help you with somethin, Sheriff?

How far is it to El Paso?

It's about a hundred and twenty miles.

You tell him I said thank you and I'll give him a call tomorrow.

Yessir.

He stopped and ate on the far side of town and sat in the booth and sipped his coffee and watched the lights out on the highway. Something wrong. He couldnt make sense out of it. He looked at his watch. 1:20. He paid and walked out and got in the cruiser and sat there. Then he drove to the intersection and turned east and drove back to the motel again.

Chigurh checked into a motel on the eastbound interstate and walked out across a windy field in the dark and watched across the highway through a pair of binoculars. The big overland trucks loomed up in the glasses and drew away. He squatted on his heels with his elbows on his knees, watching. Then he went back to the motel.

He set his alarm for one oclock and when it went off he got up and showered and dressed and walked out to his truck with his small leather bag and put it behind the seat.

He parked in the motel parking lot and he sat there for some time. Leaning back in the seat and watching in the rearview mirror. Nothing. The police cars were long gone. The yellow police tape across the door lifted in the wind and the trucks droned past headed for Arizona and California. He got out and walked up to the door and blew out the lock with his stungun and walked in and shut the door behind him. He could see the room pretty well by the light through the windows. Small spills of light from the bulletholes in the plywood door. He pulled the little bedside table over to the wall and stood and took a screwdriver from his rear pocket and began to back the screws out of the louvered steel cover of the airduct. He set it on the table and reached in and pulled out the bag and stepped down and walked over to the window and looked out at the parking lot. He took the pistol from behind his belt and opened the door and stepped out and closed it behind him and stooped under the tape and walked down to his truck and got in.

He set the bag in the floor and he'd reached for the key to turn on the ignition when he saw the Terrell County cruiser pull into the lot in front of the motel office a hundred feet away. He let go of the key and sat back. The cruiser pulled into a parking space and the lights went out. Then the motor. Chigurh waited, the pistol in his lap.

When Bell got out he took a look around the lot and then walked up to the door at 117 and tried the knob. The door was unlocked. He ducked under the tape and pushed the door open and reached and found the wallswitch and turned on the light.

The first thing he saw was the grille and the screws lying on the table. He shut the door behind him and stood there. He stepped to the window and looked past the edge of the curtain out at the parking lot. He stood there for some time.

Nothing moved. He saw something lying in the floor and stepped over and picked it up but he already knew what it was. He turned it in his hand. He walked over and sat on the bed and weighed the little piece of brass in his palm. Then he tilted it into the ashtray on the bedside table. He picked up the telephone but the line was dead. He put the receiver back in the cradle. He took his pistol from the holster and flipped open the gate and checked the shells in the cylinder and closed the gate with his thumb and sat with the pistol resting on his knee.

You dont know for sure that he's out there, he said.

Yes you do. You knew it at the restaurant. That's why you come back here.

Well what do you aim to do?

He got up and walked over and switched off the light. Five bulletholes in the door. He stood with the revolver in his hand, his thumb on the knurled hammer. Then he opened the door and walked out.

He walked to the cruiser. Studying the cars in the lot. Pickup trucks for the most part. You could always see the muzzleflash first. Just not first enough. Can you feel it when someone is watching you? A lot of people thought so. He reached the cruiser and opened the door with his left hand. The domelight came on. He stepped in and pulled the door shut and laid the pistol on the seat beside him and got out his key and put it in the ignition and started the car. Then he backed out of the parking space and switched on the lights and swung out of the lot.

When he was out of sight of the motel he pulled over onto the shoulder and took the speaker from the hook and called the sheriff's office. They sent two cars. He hung the mike up and put the cruiser in neutral and rolled back down the edge of the highway until he could just see the motel sign. He looked at his watch. 1:45. That seven minute time would make it 1:52. He waited. At the motel nothing moved. At 1:52 he saw them come down the highway and tail each other up the offramp with sirens on and lights blazing. He kept his eyes on the motel. Any vehicle that came out of the lot and headed up the access road he'd already determined to run it off the road.

When the cruisers pulled into the motel he started the car and turned on the lights and did a U-turn and went back down the road the wrong way and pulled into the lot and got out.

They went down the parking lot vehicle by vehicle with flashlights and their guns drawn and came back again. Bell was the first one back and he stood leaning against his cruiser. He nodded to the deputies. Gentlemen, he said. I think we been outgeneraled.

They holstered their pistols. He and the chief deputy walked over to the room and Bell showed him the lock and the airvent and the lock cylinder.

What's he done that with, Sheriff? the deputy said, holding the cylinder in his hand.

It's a long story, Bell said. I'm sorry to of got you all out here for nothin.

Not a problem, Sheriff.

You tell the sheriff I'll call him from El Paso.

Yessir, I'll sure do it.

Two hours later he checked into the Rodeway Inn on the east side of town and got the key and went to his room and went to bed. He woke at six as he always did and got up and closed the curtains and went back to bed but he couldnt sleep. Finally he got up and showered and dressed and went down to the coffeeshop and got his breakfast and read the paper. There'd be nothing about Moss and the girl yet. When the waitress came with more coffee he asked her what time they got the evening paper.

I dont know, she said. I quit readin it.

I dont blame you. I would if I could.

I quit readin it and I made my husband quit readin it.

Is that right?

I dont know why they call it a newspaper. I dont call that stuff news.

No.

When was the last time you read somethin about Jesus Christ in the newspaper?

Bell shook his head. I dont know, he said. I guess I'd have to say it would be a while.

I guess it would too, she said. A long while.

He'd knocked on other doors with the same sort of message, it wasnt all that new to him. He saw the window curtain move slightly and then the door opened and she stood there in jeans with her shirttail out looking at him. No expression. Just waiting. He took off his hat and she leaned against the doorjamb and turned her face away.

I'm sorry, mam, he said.

Oh God, she said. She staggered back into the room and slumped to the floor and buried her face in her forearms with her hands over her head. Bell stood there holding his hat. He didnt know what to do. He couldnt see any sign of the grandmother. Two Spanish maids were standing in the parking lot watching and whispering to each other. He stepped into the room and closed the door.

Carla Jean, he said.

Oh God, she said.

I'm just as sorry as I can be.

Oh God.

He stood there, his hat in his hand. I'm sorry, he said.

She raised her head and looked at him. Her crumpled face. Damn you, she said. You stand there and tell me you're sorry? My husband is dead. Do you understand that? You say you're sorry one more time and by God if I wont get my gun and shoot you.

IX

I had to take her at her word. Not a lot else you could do. I never saw her again. I wanted to tell her that the way they had it in the papers wasnt right. About him and that girl. It turned out she was a runaway. Fifteen years old. I dont believe that he had anything to do with her and I hate it that she thought that. Which you know she did. I called her a number of times but she'd hang up on me and I cant blame her. Then when they called me from Odessa and told me what had happened I couldnt hardly believe it. It didnt make no sense. I drove up there but there wasnt nothin to be done. Her grandmother had just died too. I tried to see if I could get his fingerprints off the FBI database but they just drew a blank. Wanted to know what his name was and what he'd done and all such as that. You end up lookin like a fool. He's a ghost. But he's out there. You wouldnt think it would be possible to just come and go thataway. I keep waitin to hear somethin else. Maybe I will yet. Or maybe not. It's easy to fool yourself. Tell yourself what you want to hear. You wake up in the night and you think about things. I aint sure anymore what it is I do want to hear. You tell yourself that maybe this business is over. But you know it aint. You can wish all you want.

My daddy always told me to just do the best you knew how and tell the truth. He said there was nothin to set a man's mind at ease like wakin up in the morning and not havin to decide who you were. And if you done somethin wrong just stand up and say you done it and say you're sorry and get on with it. Dont haul stuff around with you. I guess all that sounds pretty simple today. Even to me. All the more reason to think about it. He didnt say a lot so I tend to remember what he did say. And I dont remember that he had a lot of patience with havin to say things twice so I learned to listen the first time. I might of strayed from all of that some as a younger man but when I got back on that road I pretty much decided not to quit it again and I didnt. I think the truth is always simple. It has pretty much got to be. It needs to be simple enough for a child to understand. Otherwise it'd be too late. By the time you figured it out it would be too late.

Chigurh stood at the receptionist's desk dressed in suit and tie. He set the case in the floor at his feet and looked around the office.

How do you spell that? she said.

He told her.

Is he expecting you?

No. He's not. But he's going to be glad to see me.

Just a minute.

She buzzed the inner office. There was a silence. Then she hung the phone up. Go right in, she said.

He opened the door and walked in and a man at the desk stood up and looked at him. He came around the desk and held out his hand. I know that name, he said.

They sat on a sofa in the corner of the office and Chigurh set the case on the coffeetable and nodded at it. That's yours, he said.

What is it?

It's some money that belongs to you.

The man sat looking at the case. Then he got up and went over to the desk and leaned and pushed a button. Hold my calls, he said.

He turned and put his hands on either side of the desk behind him and leaned back and studied Chigurh. How did you find me? he said.

What difference does it make?

It makes a difference to me.

You dont have to worry. Nobody else is coming.

How do you know?

Because I'm in charge of who is coming and who is not. I think we need to address the issue here. I dont want to spend a lot of time trying to put your mind at ease. I think it would be both hopeless and thankless. So let's talk about money.

All right.

Some of it is missing. About a hundred thousand dollars. Part of that was stolen and part of it went to cover my expenses. I've been at some pains to recover your property so I'd prefer not to be addressed as some sort of bearer of bad news here. There is two point three mil in that case. I'm sorry I couldnt recover it all, but there you are.

The man hadnt moved. After a while he said: Who the hell are you?

My name is Anton Chigurh.

I know that.

Then why did you ask?

What do you want. I guess that's my question.

Well. I'd say that the purpose of my visit is simply to establish my bonafides. As someone who is an expert in a difficult field. As someone who is completely reliable and completely honest. Something like that.

Someone I might do business with.

Yes.

You're serious.

Completely.

Chigurh watched him. He watched the dilation in his eyes and the pulse in the artery of his neck. The rate of his breathing. When he'd first put his hands on the desk behind him he had looked somewhat relaxed. He was still standing in the identical attitude but he didnt look that way anymore.

There's not a bomb in that damn bag is there?

No. No bombs.

Chigurh undid the straps and unlatched the brass hasp and opened the leather flap and tipped the case forward.

Yes, the man said. Put that away.

Chigurh closed the bag. The man stood up from his leaning against the desk. He wiped his mouth with his fore-knuckle.

I think what you need to consider, Chigurh said, is how you lost this money in the first place. Who you listened to and what happened when you did.

Yes. We cant talk here.

I understand. In any case I dont expect you to absorb all of this at one sitting. I'll call you in two days time.

All right.

Chigurh rose from the couch. The man nodded toward the

case. You could do a lot of business on your own with that, he said.

Chigurh smiled. We have a lot to talk about, he said. We'll be dealing with new people now. There wont be any more problems.

What happened to the old people?

They've moved on to other things. Not everyone is suited to this line of work. The prospect of outsized profits leads people to exaggerate their own capabilities. In their minds. They pretend to themselves that they are in control of events where perhaps they are not. And it is always one's stance upon uncertain ground that invites the attentions of one's enemies. Or discourages it.

And you? What about your enemies?

I have no enemies. I dont permit such a thing.

He looked around the room. Nice office, he said. Low key. He nodded to a painting on the wall. Is that original?

The man looked at the painting. No, he said. It's not. But I own the original. I keep it in a vault.

Excellent, said Chigurh.

The funeral was on a cold and windy day in March. She stood beside her grandmother's sister. The sister's husband sat in front of her in a wheelchair with his chin resting in his hand. The dead woman had more friends than she would have reckoned. She was surprised. They'd come with their faces veiled in black. She put her hand on her uncle's shoulder and he reached up across his chest and patted it. She had thought maybe he was asleep. The whole while that the wind blew and the preacher talked she had the feeling that someone was watching her. Twice she even looked around.

It was dark when she got home. She went into the kitchen and put the kettle on and sat at the kitchen table. She hadnt felt like crying. Now she did. She lowered her face into her folded arms. Oh Mama, she said.

When she went upstairs and turned on the light in her bedroom Chigurh was sitting at the little desk waiting for her.

She stood in the doorway, her hand falling slowly away from the wallswitch. He moved not at all. She stood there, holding her hat. Finally she said: I knowed this wasnt done with.

Smart girl.

I aint got it.

Got what?

I need to set down.

Chigurh nodded toward the bed. She sat and put her hat on the bed beside her and then picked it up again and held it to her.

Too late, Chigurh said.

I know.

What is it that you havent got?

I think you know what I'm talkin about.

How much do you have.

I dont have none of it. I had about seven thousand dollars all told and I can tell you it's been long gone and they's bills aplenty left to pay yet. I buried my mother today. I aint paid for that neither.

I wouldnt worry about it.

She looked at the bedside table.

It's not there, he said.

She sat slumped forward, holding her hat in her arms. You've got no cause to hurt me, she said.

I know. But I gave my word.

Your word?

Yes. We're at the mercy of the dead here. In this case your husband.

That dont make no sense.

I'm afraid it does.

I dont have the money. You know I aint got it.

I know.

You give your word to my husband to kill me?

Yes.

He's dead. My husband is dead.

Yes. But I'm not.

You dont owe nothin to dead people.

Chigurh cocked his head slightly. No? he said.

How can you?

How can you not?

They're dead.

Yes. But my word is not dead. Nothing can change that.

You can change it.

I dont think so. Even a nonbeliever might find it useful to model himself after God. Very useful, in fact.

You're just a blasphemer.

Hard words. But what's done cannot be undone. I think you understand that. Your husband, you may be distressed to learn, had the opportunity to remove you from harm's way and he chose not to do so. He was given that option and his answer was no. Otherwise I would not be here now.

You aim to kill me.

I'm sorry.

She put the hat down on the bed and turned and looked out the window. The new green of the trees in the light of the vaporlamp in the yard bending and righting again in the evening wind. I dont know what I ever done, she said. I truly dont.

Chigurh nodded. Probably you do, he said. There's a reason for everything.

She shook her head. How many times I've said them very words. I wont again.

You've suffered a loss of faith.

I've suffered a loss of everthing I ever had. My husband wanted to kill me?

Yes. Is there anything that you'd like to say?

To who?

I'm the only one here.

I dont have nothin to say to you.

You'll be all right. Try not to worry about it.

What?

I see your look, he said. It doesn't make any difference what sort of person I am, you know. You shouldnt be more frightened to die because you think I'm a bad person.

I knowed you was crazy when I seen you settin there, she said. I knowed exactly what was in store for me. Even if I couldnt of said it.

Chigurh smiled. It's a hard thing to understand, he said. I see people struggle with it. The look they get. They always say the same thing.

What do they say.

They say: You dont have to do this.

You dont.

It's not any help though, is it?

No.

So why do you say it?

I aint never said it before.

Any of you.

There's just me, she said. There aint nobody else.

Yes. Of course.

She looked at the gun. She turned away. She sat with her head down, her shoulders shaking. Oh Mama, she said.

None of this was your fault.

She shook her head, sobbing.

You didnt do anything. It was bad luck.

She nodded.

He watched her, his chin in his hand. All right, he said. This is the best I can do.

He straightened out his leg and reached into his pocket and drew out a few coins and took one and held it up. He turned it. For her to see the justice of it. He held it between his thumb and forefinger and weighed it and then flipped it spinning in the air and caught it and slapped it down on his wrist. Call it, he said.

She looked at him, at his outheld wrist. What? She said.

Call it.

I wont do it.

Yes you will. Call it.

God would not want me to do that.

Of course he would. You should try to save yourself. Call it. This is your last chance.

Heads, she said.

He lifted his hand away. The coin was tails.

I'm sorry.

She didnt answer.

Maybe it's for the best.

She looked away. You make it like it was the coin. But you're the one.

It could have gone either way.

The coin didnt have no say. It was just you.

Perhaps. But look at it my way. I got here the same way the coin did.

She sat sobbing softly. She didnt answer.

For things at a common destination there is a common path. Not always easy to see. But there.

Everthing I ever thought has turned out different, she said. There aint the least part of my life I could of guessed. Not this, not none of it.

I know.

You wouldnt of let me off noway.

I had no say in the matter. Every moment in your life is a turning and every one a choosing. Somewhere you made a choice. All followed to this. The accounting is scrupulous. The shape is drawn. No line can be erased. I had no belief in your ability to move a coin to your bidding. How could you? A person's path through the world seldom changes and even more seldom will it change abruptly. And the shape of your path was visible from the beginning.

She sat sobbing. She shook her head.

Yet even though I could have told you how all of this would end I thought it not too much to ask that you have a final glimpse of hope in the world to lift your heart before the shroud drops, the darkness. Do you see?

Oh God, she said. Oh God.

I'm sorry.

She looked at him a final time. You dont have to, she said. You dont. You dont.

He shook his head. You're asking that I make myself vulnerable and that I can never do. I have only one way to live. It doesnt allow for special cases. A coin toss perhaps. In this case to small purpose. Most people dont believe that there can be such a person. You can see what a problem that must be for them. How to prevail over that which you refuse to acknowledge the existence of. Do you understand? When I came into your life your life was over. It had a beginning, a middle, and an end. This is the end. You can say that things could have turned out differently. That they could have been some other way. But what does that mean? They are not some other way. They are this way. You're asking that I second say the world. Do you see?

Yes, she said, sobbing. I do. I truly do.

Good, he said. That's good. Then he shot her.

The car that hit Chigurh in the intersection three blocks from the house was a ten year old Buick that had run a stop-sign. There were no skidmarks at the site and the vehicle had made no attempt to brake. Chigurh never wore a seatbelt driving in the city because of just such hazards and although he saw the vehicle coming and threw himself to the other side of the truck the impact carried the caved-in driver side door to him instantly and broke his arm in two places and broke some ribs and cut his head and his leg. He crawled out of the passenger side door and staggered to the sidewalk and sat in the grass of someone's lawn and looked at his arm. Bone sticking up under the skin. Not good. A woman in a housedress ran out screaming.

Blood kept running into his eyes and he tried to think. He held the arm and turned it and tried to see how badly it was bleeding. If the median artery were severed. He thought not. His head was ringing. No pain. Not yet.

Two teenage boys were standing there looking at him.

Are you all right, mister?

Yeah, he said. I'm all right. Let me just sit here a minute.

There's an ambulance comin. Man over yonder went to call one.

All right.

You sure you're all right.

Chigurh looked at them. What will you take for that shirt? he said.

They looked at each other. What shirt?

Any damn shirt. How much?

He straightened out his leg and reached in his pocket and got out his moneyclip. I need something to wrap around my head and I need a sling for this arm.

One of the boys began to unbutton his shirt. Hell, mister. Why didnt you say so? I'll give you my shirt.

Chigurh took the shirt and bit into it and ripped it in two down the back. He wrapped his head in a bandanna and he twisted the other half of the shirt into a sling and put his arm in it.

Tie this for me, he said.

They looked at each other.

Just tie it.

The boy in the T-shirt stepped forward and knelt and knotted the sling. That arm dont look good, he said.

Chigurh thumbed a bill out of the clip and put the clip back in his pocket and took the bill from between his teeth and got to his feet and held it out.

Hell, mister. I dont mind helpin somebody out. That's a lot of money.

Take it. Take it and you dont know what I looked like. You hear?

The boy took the bill. Yessir, he said.

They watched him set off up the sidewalk, holding the twist of the bandanna against his head, limping slightly. Part of that's mine, the other boy said.

You still got your damn shirt.

That aint what it was for.

That may be, but I'm still out a shirt.

They walked out into the street where the vehicles sat steaming. The streetlamps had come on. A pool of green antifreeze was collecting in the gutter. When they passed the open door of Chigurh's truck the one in the T-shirt stopped the other with his hand. You see what I see? he said.

Shit, the other one said.

What they saw was Chigurh's pistol lying in the floorboard of the truck. They could already hear the sirens in the distance. Get it, the first one said. Go on.

Why me?

I aint got a shirt to cover it with. Go on. Hurry.

He climbed the three wooden steps to the porch and tapped loosely at the door with the back of his hand. He took off his hat and pressed his shirtsleeve against his forehead and put his hat back on again.

Come in, a voice called.

He opened the door and stepped into the cool darkness. Ellis?

I'm back here. Come on back.

He walked through to the kitchen. The old man was sitting beside the table in his chair. The room smelled of old bacon-grease and stale woodsmoke from the stove and over it all lay a faint tang of urine. Like the smell of cats but it wasnt just cats. Bell stood in the doorway and took his hat off. The old man looked up at him. One clouded eye from a cholla spine where a horse had thrown him years ago. Hey, Ed Tom, he said. I didnt know who that was.

How are you makin it?

You're lookin at it. You by yourself?

Yessir.

Set down. You want some coffee?

Bell looked at the clutter on the checked oilcloth. Bottles

of medicine. Breadcrumbs. Quarterhorse magazines. Thank you no, he said. I appreciate it.

I had a letter from your wife.

You can call her Loretta.

I know I can. Did you know she writes me?

I guess I knew she'd wrote you a time or two.

It's more than a time or two. She writes pretty regular. Tells me the family news.

I didnt know there was any.

You might be surprised.

So what was special about this letter then.

She just told me you was quittin, that's all. Set down.

The old man didnt watch to see if he would or he wouldnt. He fell to rolling himself a cigarette from a sack of tobacco at his elbow. He twisted the end in his mouth and turned it around and lit it with an old Zippo lighter worn through to the brass. He sat smoking, holding the cigarette pencilwise in his fingers.

Are you all right? Bell said.

I'm all right.

He wheeled the chair slightly sideways and watched Bell through the smoke. I got to say you look older, he said.

I am older.

The old man nodded. Bell had pulled out a chair and sat and he put his hat on the table.

Let me ask you somethin, he said.

All right.

What's your biggest regret in life.

The old man looked at him, gauging the question. I dont know, he said. I aint got all that many regrets. I could imagine lots of things that you might think would make a man happier. I reckon bein able to walk around might be one. You can make up your own list. You might even have one. I think by the time you're grown you're as happy as you're goin to be. You'll have good times and bad times, but in the end you'll be about as happy as you was before. Or as unhappy. I've knowed people that just never did get the hang of it.

I know what you mean.

I know you do.

The old man smoked. If what you're askin me is what made me the unhappiest then I think you already know that.

Yessir.

And it aint this chair. And it aint this cotton eye.

Yessir. I know that.

You sign on for the ride you probably think you got at least some notion of where the ride's goin. But you might not. Or you might of been lied to. Probably nobody would blame you then. If you quit. But if it's just that it turned out to be a little roughern what you had in mind. Well. That's somethin else.

Bell nodded.

I guess some things are better not put to the test.

I guess that's right.

What would it take to run Loretta off?

I dont know. I guess I'd have to do somethin that was

pretty bad. It damn sure wouldnt be just cause things got a little rough. She's done been there a time or two.

Ellis nodded. He tipped the ash from his smoke into a jar-lid on the table. I'll take your word on that, he said.

Bell smiled. He looked around. How fresh is that coffee?

I think it's all right. I generally make a fresh pot here ever week even if there is some left over.

Bell smiled again and rose and carried the pot to the counter and plugged it in.

They sat at the table drinking coffee out of the same crazed porcelain cups that had been in that house since before he was born. Bell looked at the cup and he looked around the kitchen. Well, he said. Some things dont change, I reckon.

What would that be? the old man said.

Hell, I dont know.

I dont either.

How many cats you got?

Several. Depends on what you mean by got. Some of em are half wild and the rest are just outlaws. They run out the door when they heard your truck.

Did you hear the truck?

How's that?

I said did you . . . You're havin a little fun with me.

What give you that idea?

Did you?

No. I seen the cats skedaddle.

You want some more of this?

I'm done.

The man that shot you died in prison.

In Angola. Yes.

What would you of done if he'd been released?

I dont know. Nothin. There wouldnt be no point to it. There aint no point to it. Not to any of it.

I'm kindly surprised to hear you say that.

You wear out, Ed Tom. All the time you spend tryin to get back what's been took from you there's more goin out the door. After a while you just try and get a tourniquet on it. Your grandad never asked me to sign on as deputy with him. I done that my own self. Hell, I didnt have nothin else to do. Paid about the same as cowboyin. Anyway, you never know what worse luck your bad luck has saved you from. I was too young for one war and too old for the next one. But I seen what come out of it. You can be patriotic and still believe that some things cost more than what they're worth. Ask them Gold Star mothers what they paid and what they got for it. You always pay too much. Particularly for promises. There aint no such thing as a bargain promise. You'll see. Maybe you done have.

Bell didnt answer.

I always thought when I got older that God would sort of come into my life in some way. He didnt. I dont blame him. If I was him I'd have the same opinion about me that he does.

You dont know what he thinks.

Yes I do.

He looked at Bell. I can remember one time you come to

see me after you all had moved to Denton. You walked in and you looked around and you asked me what I intended to do.

All right.

You wouldnt ask me now though, would you?

Maybe not.

You wouldnt.

He sipped the rank black coffee.

You ever think about Harold? Bell said.

Harold?

Yes.

Not much. He was some older than me. He was born in ninety-nine. Pretty sure that's right. What made you think about Harold?

I was readin some of your mother's letters to him, that's all. I just wondered what you remembered about him.

Was they any letters from him?

No.

You think about your family. Try to make sense out of all that. I know what it did to my mother. She never got over it. I dont know what sense any of that makes either. You know that gospel song? We'll understand it all by and by? That takes a lot of faith. You think about him goin over there and dyin in a ditch somewheres. Seventeen year old. You tell me. Because I damn sure dont know.

I hear you. Did you want to go somewheres?

I dont need nobody haulin me around. I aim to just set right here. I'm fine, Ed Tom.

It aint no trouble.

I know it.

All right.

Bell watched him. The old man stubbed out his cigarette in the lid. Bell tried to think about his life. Then he tried not to. You aint turned infidel have you Uncle Ellis?

No. No. Nothin like that.

Do you think God knows what's happenin?

I expect he does.

You think he can stop it?

No. I dont.

They sat quietly at the table. After a while the old man said: She mentioned there was a lot of old pictures and family stuff. What to do about that. Well. There aint nothin to do about it I dont reckon. Is there?

No. I dont reckon there is.

I told her to send Uncle Mac's old cinco peso badge and his thumb-buster to the Rangers. I believe they got a museum. But I didnt know what to tell her. There's all that stuff here. In the chifforobe in yonder. That rolltop desk is full of papers. He tilted the cup and looked into the bottom of it.

He never rode with Coffee Jack. Uncle Mac. That's all bull. I dont know who started that. He was shot down on his own porch in Hudspeth County.

That's what I always heard.

They was seven or eight of em come to the house. Wantin this and wantin that. He went back in the house and come out with a shotgun but they was way ahead of him and they shot him down in his own doorway. She run out and tried to stop the bleedin. Tried to get him back in the house. Said he kept tryin to get hold of the shotgun again. They just set there on their horses. Finally left. I dont know why. Somethin scared em, I reckon. One of em said somethin in injun and they all turned and left out. They never come in the house or nothin. She got him inside but he was a big man and they was no way she could of got him up in the bed. She fixed a pallet on the floor. Wasnt nothin to be done. She always said she should of just left him there and rode for help but I dont know where it was she would of rode to. He wouldnt of let her go noway. Wouldnt hardly let her go in the kitchen. He knew what the score was if she didnt. He was shot through the right lung. And that was that. As they say.

When did he die?

Eighteen and seventy-nine.

No, I mean was it right away or in the night or when was it.

I believe it was that night. Or early of the mornin. She buried him herself. Diggin in that hard caliche. Then she just packed the wagon and hitched the horses and pulled out of there and she never did go back. That house burned down sometime back in the twenties. What hadnt fell down. I could take you to it today. The rock chimney used to be standin and it may be yet. There was a good bit of land proved up on. Eight or ten sections if I remember. She couldnt pay the taxes on it, little as they was. Couldnt sell it. Did you remember her?

No. I seen a photograph of me and her when I was about four. She's settin in a rocker on the porch of this house and I'm standin alongside of her. I wish I could say I remember her but I dont.

She never did remarry. Later years she was a school-teacher. San Angelo. This country was hard on people. But they never seemed to hold it to account. In a way that seems peculiar. That they didnt. You think about what all has happened to just this one family. I dont know what I'm doin here still knockin around. All them young people. We dont know where half of em is even buried at. You got to ask what was the good in all that. So I go back to that. How come people dont feel like this country has got a lot to answer for? They dont. You can say that the country is just the country, it dont actively do nothin, but that dont mean much. I seen a man shoot his pickup truck with a shotgun one time. He must of thought it done somethin. This country will kill you in a heartbeat and still people love it. You understand what I'm sayin?

I think I do. Do you love it?

I guess you could say I do. But I'd be the first one to tell you I'm as ignorant as a box of rocks so you sure dont want to go by nothin I'd say.

Bell smiled. He got up and went to the sink. The old man

turned the chair slightly to where he could see him. What are you doin? he said.

I thought I'd just wash these here dishes.

Hell, leave em, Ed Tom. Lupe'll be here in the mornin.

It wont take but a minute.

The water from the tap was gypwater. He filled the sink and added a scoop of soap powder. Then he added another.

I thought you used to have a television set in here.

I used to have a lot of things.

Why didnt you say somethin? I'll get you one.

I dont need one.

Keep you company some.

It didnt quit on me. I throwed it out.

You dont never watch the news?

No. Do you?

Not much.

He rinsed the dishes and left them to drain and stood looking out the window at the little weedgrown yard. A weathered smokehouse. An aluminum two horse trailer on blocks. You used to have chickens, he said.

Yep, the old man said.

Bell dried his hands and came back to the table and sat. He looked at his uncle. Did you ever do anything you was ashamed of to the point where you never would tell nobody?

His uncle thought about that. I'd say I have, he said. I'd say about anybody has. What is it you've found out about me?

I'm serious.

All right.

I mean somethin bad.

How bad.

I dont know. Where it stuck with you.

Like somethin you could go to jail for?

Well, it could be somethin like that I reckon. It wouldnt have to be.

I'd have to think about that.

No you wouldnt.

What's got into you? I aint goin to invite you out here no more.

You didnt invite me this time.

Well. That's true.

Bell sat with his elbows on the table and his hands folded together. His uncle watched him. I hope you aint fixin to make some terrible confession, he said. I might not want to hear it.

Do you want to hear it?

Yeah. Go ahead.

All right.

It aint of a sexual nature is it?

No.

That's all right. Go ahead and tell it anyways.

It's about bein a war hero.

All right. Would that be you?

Yeah. That'd be me.

Go ahead.

I'm tryin to. This is actually what happened. What got me that commendation.

Go ahead.

We was in a forward position monitorin radio signals and we was holed up in a farmhouse. Just a two room stone house. We'd been there two days and it never did quit rainin. Rained like all get-out. Somewhere about the middle of the second day the radio operator had took his headset off and he said: Listen. Well, we did. When somebody said listen you listened. And we didnt hear nothin. And I said: What is it? And he said: Nothin.

I said What the hell are you talkin about, nothin? What did you hear? And he said: I mean you cant hear nothin. Listen. And he was right. There was not a sound nowheres. No field-piece or nothin. All you could hear was the rain. And that was about the last thing I remember. When I woke up I was layin outside in the rain and I dont know how long I'd been layin there. I was wet and cold and my ears was ringin and whenever I set up and looked the house was gone. Just part of the wall at one end was standin was all. A mortarshell had come through the wall and just blowed it all to hell. Well, I couldnt hear a thing. I couldnt hear the rain or nothin. If I said somethin I could hear it inside my head but that was all. I got up and walked over to where the house was and there was sections of the roof layin over a good part of it and I seen one of our men buried in them rocks and timbers and I tried to move some stuff to see if I couldnt get to him. My whole head just felt numb. And while I was doin that I raised up and looked out and here come these German riflemen across this field. They was comin out of a patch of woods about two hundred yards off and comin across this field. I still didnt know exactly what had happened. I was kindly in a daze. I crouched down there by the side of the wall and the first thing I seen was Wallace's .30 caliber stickin out from under some timbers. That thing was aircooled and it was belt fed out of a metal box and I figured if I let em run up a little more on me I could operate on em out there in the open and they wouldnt call in another round cause they'd be too close. I scratched around and finally got that thing dug out, it and the tripod, and I dug around some more and come up with the ammo box for it and I got set up behind the section of wall there and jacked back the slide and pushed off the safety and here we went.

It was hard to tell where the rounds was hittin on account of the ground bein wet but I knew I was doin some good. I emptied out about two feet of belt and I kept watchin out there and after it'd been quiet two or three minutes one of them krauts jumped up and tried to make a run for the woods but I was ready for that. I kept the rest of em pinned down and all the while I could hear some of our men groanin and I sure didnt know what I was goin to do come dark. And that's what they give me the Bronze Star for. The major that put me in for it was named McAllister and he was from Georgia. And I told him I didnt want it. And he just set there lookin at me and directly he said: I'm waitin on you to tell me your reasons for wantin to refuse a military commendation. So I told him. And when I got done he said: Sergeant, you will accept the commendation. I guess they had to make it look good. Look like it counted for somethin. Losin the position. He said you will accept it and if you tell it around what you told me it will get back to me and when it does you are goin to wish you was in hell with your back broke. Is that clear? And I said yessir. Said that was about as clear as you could make it. So that was it.

So now you're fixin to tell me what you done.

Yessir.

When it got dark.

When it got dark. Yessir.

What did you do?

I cut and run.

The old man thought about that. After a while he said: I got to assume that it seemed like a pretty good idea at the time.

Yeah, Bell said. It did.

What would of happened if you'd stayed there?

They'd of come up in the dark and lobbed grenades in on me. Or maybe gone back up in the woods and called in another round.

Yeah.

Bell sat there with his hands crossed on the oilcloth. He

looked at his uncle. The old man said: I aint sure what it is you're askin me.

I aint either.

You left your buddies behind.

Yeah.

You didnt have no choice.

I had a choice. I could of stayed.

You couldnt of helped em.

Probably not. I thought about takin that .30 caliber off about a hundred feet or so and waitin till they throwed their grenades or whatever. Lettin em come on up. I could of killed a few more. Even in the dark. I dont know. I set there and watched it come night. Pretty sunset. It had done cleared up by then. Had finally quit rainin. That field had been sowed in oats and there was just the stalks. Fall of the year. I watched it get dark and I had not heard nothin from anybody that was in the wreckage there for a while. They might could of all been dead by then. But I didnt know that. And quick as it got dark I got up and I left out of there. I didnt even have a gun. I dang sure wasnt haulin that .30 caliber with me. My head had quit hurtin some and I could even hear a little. It had quit rainin but I was wet through and I was cold to where my teeth was chatterin. I could make out the dipper and I headed due west as near as I could make it and I just kept goin. I passed a house or two but there wasnt nobody around. It was a battle-zone, that country. People had just left out. Come daylight I laid up in a patch of woods. What woods it was. That whole country looked like a burn. Just the treetrunks was all that was left. And sometime that next night I come to an American position and that was pretty much it. I thought after so many years it would go away. I dont know why I thought that. Then I thought that maybe I could make up for it and I reckon that's what I have tried to do.

They sat. After a while the old man said: Well, in all honesty I cant see it bein all that bad. Maybe you ought to ease up on yourself some.

Maybe. But you go into battle it's a blood oath to look after the men with you and I dont know why I didnt. I wanted to. When you're called on like that you have to make up your mind that you'll live with the consequences. But you dont know what the consequences will be. You end up layin a lot of things at your own door that you didnt plan on. If I was supposed to die over there doin what I'd give my word to do then that's what I should of done. You can tell it any way you want but that's the way it is. I should of done it and I didnt. And some part of me has never quit wishin I could go back. And I cant. I didnt know you could steal your own life. And I didnt know that it would bring you no more benefit than about anything else you might steal. I think I done the best with it I knew how but it still wasnt mine. It never has been.

The old man sat for a long time. He was bent slightly forward looking at the floor. After a while he nodded. I think I know where this is goin, he said.

Yessir.

What do you think he would of done?

I know what he would of done.

Yeah. I guess I do too.

He'd of set there till hell froze over and then stayed a while on the ice.

Do you think that makes him a better man than you?

Yessir. I do.

I might could tell you some things about him that would change your mind. I knew him pretty good.

Well sir, I doubt that you could. With all due respect. Besides which I doubt that you would.

I aint. But then I might say that he lived in different times. Had Jack of been born fifty years later he might of had a different view of things.

You might. But nobody in this room would believe it.

Yeah, I expect that's true. He looked up at Bell. What did you tell me for?

I think I just needed to unload my wagon.

You waited long enough about doin it.

Yessir. Maybe I needed to hear it myself. I'm not the man of an older time they say I am. I wish I was. I'm a man of this time.

Or maybe this was just a practice run.

Maybe.

You aim to tell her?

Yessir, I guess I do.

Well.

What do you think she'll say?

Well, I expect you might come out of it a little better than what you think.

Yessir, Bell said. I surely hope so.

X

He said I was bein hard on myself. Said it was a sign of old age. Tryin to set things right. I guess there's some truth to that. But it aint the whole truth. I agreed with him that there wasnt a whole lot good you could say about old age and he said he knew one thing and I said what is that. And he said it dont last long. I waited for him to smile but he didnt. I said well, that's pretty cold. And he said it was no colder than what the facts called for. So that was all there was about that. I knew what he'd say anyways, bless his heart. You care about people you try and lighten their load for em. Even when it's self-ordained. The other thing that was on my mind I never even got around to but I believe it to be related because I believe that whatever you do in your life it will get back to you. If you live long enough it will. And I can think of no reason in the world for that no-good to of killed that girl. What did she ever do to him? The truth is I never should of gone up there in the first place. Now they got that Mexican up here in Huntsville for killin that state trooper that he shot him and set his car afire and him in it and I dont believe he done it. But that's what he's goin to get the death penalty for. So what is my obligation there? I think I have sort of waited for all of this to go away somehow or another and of course it aint. I think I knew that when it started. It had that feel to it. Like I was fixin to get drug into somethin where the road back was goin to be a pretty long one.

When he asked me why this come up now after so many years I said that it had always been there. That I had just ignored it for the most part. But he's right, it did come up. I think sometimes people would rather have a bad answer about things than no answer at all. When I told it, well it took a shape I would not have guessed it to have and in that way he was right too. It was like a ballplayer told me one time he said that if he had some slight injury and it bothered him a little bit, nagged at him, he generally played better. It kept his mind focused on one thing instead of a hundred. I can understand that. Not that it changes anything.

I thought if I lived my life in the strictest way I knew how then I would not ever again have a thing that would eat on me thataway. I said that I was twenty-one years old and I was entitled to one mistake, particularly if I could learn from it and become the sort of man I had it in my mind to be. Well, I was wrong about all of that. Now I aim to quit and a good part of it is just knowin that I wont be called on to hunt this man. I reckon he's a man. So you could say to me that I aint changed a bit and I dont know that I would even have a argument about that. Thirty-six years. That's a painful thing to know.

One other thing he said. You'd think a man that had waited eighty some odd years on God to come into his life, well, you'd think he'd come. If he didnt you'd still have to figure that he knew what he was doin. I dont know what other description of God you could have. So what you end up with is that those he has spoke to are the ones that must of needed it the worst. That's not a easy thing to accept. Particularly as it might apply to someone like Loretta. But then maybe we are all of us lookin through the wrong end of the glass. Always have been.

Aunt Carolyn's letters to Harold. The reason she had them letters was that he had saved em. She was the one raised him and she was the same as his mother. Them letters was dog-eared and tore and covered with mud and I dont know what all. The thing about them letters. Well for one thing you could tell they were just country people. I dont think he'd ever been out of Irion County, let alone the State of Texas. But the thing about them letters was you could tell that the world she was plannin on him comin back to was not ever goin to be here. Easy to see now. Sixty some years on. But they just had no notion at all. You can say you like it or you dont like it but it dont change nothin. I've told my deputies more than once that you fix what you can fix and you let the rest go. If there aint nothin to be done about it it aint even a problem. It's just a aggravation. And the truth is I dont have no more idea of the world that is brewin out there than what Harold did.

Of course as it turned out he never come home at all. There was not nothin in them letters to suggest that she had reckoned on that possibility.

Well, you know she did. She just wouldnt of said nothin about it to him.

I've still got that medal of course. It come in a fancy purple box with a ribbon and all. It was in my bureau for years and then one day I took it out and put it in the drawer in the livin room table where I wouldnt have to look at it. Not that I ever looked at it, but it was there. Harold didnt get no medal. He just come home in a wooden box. And I dont believe they had Gold Star mothers in the First World War but if they had of Aunt Carolyn would not of got one of them either since he was not her natural son. But she should of. She never got his war pension neither.

So. I went back out there one more time. I walked over that ground and there was very little sign that anything had ever took place there. I picked up a shellcasin or two. That was about it. I stood out there a long time and I thought about things. It was one of them warm days you get in the winter sometimes. A little wind. I still keep thinkin maybe it is somethin about the country. Sort of the way Ellis said. I thought about my family and about him out there in his wheelchair in the old house and it just seemed to me that this country has got a strange kind of history and a damned bloody one too.

About anywhere you care to look. I could stand back off and smile about such thoughts as them but I still have em. I dont make excuses for the way I think. Not no more. I talk to my daughter. She would be thirty now. That's all right. I dont care how that sounds. I like talkin to her. Call it superstition or whatever you want. I know that over the years I have give her the heart I always wanted for myself and that's all right. That's why I listen to her. I know I'll always get the best from her. It dont get mixed up with my own ignorance or my own meanness. I know how that sounds and I guess I'd have to say that I dont care. I never even told my wife and we dont have a whole lot of secrets from one another. I dont think she'd say I'm crazy, but some might. Ed Tom? Yeah, they had to swear out a lunacy warrant. I hear they're feedin him under the door. That's all right. I listen to what she says and what she says makes good sense. I wish she'd say more of it. I can use all the help I can get. Well, that's enough of that.

When he walked in the house the phone was ringing. Sheriff Bell, he said. He made his way to the sideboard and picked up the phone. Sheriff Bell, he said.

Sheriff this is Detective Cook with the Odessa police.

Yessir.

There's a report we have here that is flagged with your name. It has to do with a woman named Carla Jean Moss that was murdered here back in March.

Yessir. I appreciate you callin.

They picked up the murder weapon off of the FBI ballistics database and they traced it down to a boy here in Midland. The boy says he got the gun out of a truck at a accident scene. Just seen it and took it. And I expect that's right. I talked to him. He sold it and it turned up in a convenience store robbery in Shreveport Louisiana. Now the accident where he got the gun, it took place on the same day as the murder did. The man that owned the gun left it in the truck and disappeared and he aint been heard from since. So you can see where this is goin. We dont get a lot of unsolved homicides up here and we damn sure dont like em. Can I ask you what was your interest in the case, Sheriff?

Bell told him. Cook listened. Then he gave him a number. It was the investigator of the accident. Roger Catron. Let me call him first. He'll talk to you.

That's all right, Bell said. He'll talk to me. I've known him for years.

He called the number and Catron answered.

How're you doin Ed Tom.

I aint braggin.

What can I do you for.

Bell told him about the wreck. Yessir, Catron said. Sure I remember it. There was two boys killed in that wreck. We still aint found the driver of the other vehicle.

What happened?

Boys'd been smokin dope. They run a stopsign and hit a brand new Dodge pickup broadside. Totaled it out. The old boy in the pickup he climbed out and just took off up the street. Fore we got there. Truck had been bought in Mexico. Illegal. No EPA or nothin. No registration.

What about the other vehicle.

There was three boys in it. Nineteen, twenty years old. All of em Mexican. The only one lived was the one in the back seat. Apparently they was passin around a doober and they went through this intersection probably about sixty mile a hour and just T-boned the old boy in the truck. The one in the passenger side of the car, he come through the windscreen head first and crossed the street and landed on a woman's porch. She was out puttin some mail in her box and he didnt miss her by much. She set off down the street in her housewrapper and haircurlers just a hollerin. I dont think she's right yet.

What did you all do with the boy that took the gun?

We cut him loose.

If I come up there you reckon I could talk to him?

I'd say you could. I'm lookin at him on the screen right now.

What's his name?

David DeMarco.

Is he Mexican?

No. The boys in the car was. Not him.

Will he talk to me?

One way to find out.

I'll be there in the mornin.

I look forward to seein you.

Catron had called the boy and talked to him and when the boy walked into the cafe he didnt seem particularly worried about anything. He slid into the booth and propped up one foot and sucked at his teeth and looked at Bell.

You want some coffee?

Yeah. I'll take some coffee.

Bell raised a finger and the waitress came over and took his order. He looked at the boy.

What I wanted to talk to you about was the man that walked away from that wreck. I wonder if there's anything that comes to mind about him. Anything you might remember.

The boy shook his head. Naw, he said. He looked around the room.

How bad was he hurt?

I dont know. It looked like his arm was broke.

What else.

Had a cut on his head. I couldnt say how bad he was hurt. He could walk.

Bell watched him. How old a man would you say he was?

Hell, Sheriff. I dont know. He was pretty bloody and all.

On the report you said he was maybe in his late thirties.

Yeah. Somethin like that.

Who were you with.

What?

Who were you with.

Wasnt with nobody.

The neighbor there who called in the report, he said there was two of you.

Well, he's full of it.

Yeah? I talked to him this mornin and he seemed to me to be about as unfull of it as they come.

The waitress brought the coffee. DeMarco poured about a quarter cup of sugar into his and and sat stirring it.

You know this man had just got done killin a woman two blocks away when he got in that wreck.

Yeah. I didnt know it at the time.

You know how many people he's killed?

I dont know nothin about him.

How tall was he would you say?

Not real tall. Sort of medium.

Was he wearin boots.

Yeah. I think he was wearin boots.

What kind of boots.

I think they might of been ostrich.

Expensive boots.

Yeah.

How badly was he bleedin?

I dont know. He was bleedin. He had a cut on his head.

What did he say?

He didnt say nothin.

What did you say to him?

Nothin. I asked him was he all right.

You think he might of died?

I got no idea.

Bell leaned back. He turned the saltcellar a half turn on the tabletop. Then he turned it back again.

Tell me who you were with.

Wasnt with nobody.

Bell studied him. The boy sucked his teeth. He picked up the coffee mug and sipped the coffee and set it down again.

You aint goin to help me, are you?

I done told you all I know to tell. You seen the report. That's all I know to tell you.

Bell sat watching him. Then he got up and put on his hat and left.

In the morning he went to the high school and got some names from DeMarco's teacher. The first one he talked to wanted to know how he'd found him. He was a big kid and he sat with his hands folded and looked down at his tennis shoes. They were about a size fourteen and had Left and Right written on the toecaps in purple ink.

There's somethin you all aint tellin me.

The boy shook his head.

Did he threaten you?

Naw.

What did he look like? Was he Mexican?

I dont think so. He was kindly dark complected is all.

Were you afraid of him?

I wasnt till you showed up. Hell, Sheriff, I knew we shouldnt of took the damn thing. It was a dumb-ass thing to do. I aint goin to set here and say it was David's idea even if it was. I'm big enough to say no.

Yes you are.

It was all just weird. Them boys in the car was dead. Am I in trouble over this?

What else did he say to you.

The boy looked around the lunchroom. He looked almost in tears. If I had it to do over again I'd do it different. I know that.

What did he say.

He said that we didnt know what he looked like. He give David a hundred dollar bill.

A hundred dollars.

Yeah. David give him his shirt. To make a sling for his arm.

Bell nodded. All right. What did he look like.

He was medium height. Medium build. Looked like he was in shape. In his mid thirties maybe. Dark hair. Dark brown, I think. I dont know, Sheriff. He looked like anybody.

Like anybody.

The kid looked at his shoes. He looked up at Bell. He didnt look like anybody. I mean there wasnt nothin unusual lookin about him. But he didnt look like anybody you'd want to mess with. When he said somethin you damn sure listened. There was a bone stickin out under the skin on his arm and he didnt pay no more attention to it than nothin.

All right.

Am I in trouble over this?

No.

I appreciate it.

You dont know where things will take you, do you?

No sir, you dont. I think I learned somethin from it. If that's any use to you.

It is. Do you think DeMarco learned anything?

The boy shook his head. I dont know, he said. I cant speak for David.

XI

I got Molly to run down his relatives and we finally found his dad in San Saba. I left to go up there on a Friday evenin and I remember thinkin to myself when I left that this was probably another dumb thing I was fixin to do but I went anyways. I'd done talked to him on the phone. He didnt sound like he was waitin to see me or he wasnt waitin but he said to come on so here I went. Checked in a motel when I got there and drove out to his house in the mornin.

His wife had died some years back. We set out on the porch and drunk iced tea and I guess we'd of set there from now on if I hadnt of said somethin. He was a bit oldern me. Ten years maybe. I told him what I'd come to tell him. About his boy. Told him the facts. He just set there and nodded. He was settin in a swing and he just rocked back and forth a little and held that glass of tea in his lap. I didnt know what else to say so I just shut up and we set there for quite some time. And then he said, and he didnt look at me, he just looked out across the yard, and he said: He was the best rifleshot I ever saw. Bar none. I didnt know what to say. I said: Yessir.

He was a sniper in Vietnam you know.

I said I didnt know that.

He was not in no drug deals.

No sir. He was not.

He nodded. He wasnt raised that way, he said.

Yessir.

Was you in the war?

Yes I was. European theatre.

He nodded. Llewelyn when he come home he went to visit several families of buddies of his that had not made it back. He give it up. He didnt know what to say to em. He said he could see em settin there lookin at him and wishin he was dead. You could see it in their faces. In the place of their own loved one, you understand.

Yessir. I can understand that.

I can too. But aside from that they'd all done things over there that they'd just as soon left over there. We didnt have nothin like that in the war. Or very little of it. He smacked the tar out of one or two of them hippies. Spittin on him. Callin him a babykiller. A lot of them boys that come back, they're still havin problems. I thought it was because they didnt have the country behind em. But I think it might be worse than that even. The country they did have was in pieces. It still is. It wasnt the hippies' fault. It wasnt the fault of them boys that got sent over there neither. Eighteen, nineteen year old.

He turned and looked at me. And then I thought he looked a lot older. His eyes looked old. He said: People will tell you it was Vietnam brought this country to its knees. But I never believed that. It was already in bad shape. Vietnam was just the icin on the cake. We didnt have nothin to give to em to take over there. If we'd sent em without rifles I dont know as they'd ofbeen all that much worse off. You cant go to war like that. You cant go to war without God. I dont know what is goin to happen when the next one comes. I surely dont.

And that was pretty much all that was said. I thanked him for his time. The next day was goin to be my last day in the office and I had a good deal to think about. I drove back to I-10 along the back roads. Drove down to Cherokee and took 501. I tried to put things in perspective but sometimes you're just too close to it. It's a life's work to see yourself for what you really are and even then you might be wrong. And that is somethin I dont want to be wrong about. I've thought about why it was I wanted to be a lawman. There was always some part of me that wanted to be in charge. Pretty much insisted on it. Wanted people to listen to what I had to say. But there was a part of me too that just wanted to pull everbody back in the boat. If I've tried to cultivate anything it's been that. I think we are all of us ill prepared for what is to come and I dont care what shape it takes. And whatever comes my guess is that it will have small power to sustain us. These old people I talk to, if you could of told em that there would be people on the streets of our Texas towns with green hair and bones in their noses speakin a language they couldnt even understand, well, they just flat out wouldnt of believed you. But what if you'd of told em it was their own grandchildren? Well, all of that is signs and wonders but it dont tell you how it got that way. And it dont tell you nothin about how it's fixin to get, neither. Part of it was I always thought I could at least someway put things right and I guess I just dont feel that way no more. I dont know what I do feel like. I feel like them old people I was talkin about. Which aint goin to get better neither. I'm bein asked to stand for somethin that I dont have the same belief in it I once did. Asked to believe in somethin I might not hold with the way I once did. That's the problem. I failed at it even when I did. Now I've seen it held to the light. Seen any number of believers fall away. I've been forced to look at it again and I've been forced to look at myself. For better or for worse I do not know. I dont know that I would even advise you to throw in with me, and I never had them sorts of doubts before. If I'm wiser in the ways of the world it come at a price. Pretty good price too. When I told her I was quittin she at first didnt take me to mean it literally but I told her I did so mean it. I told her I hoped the people of this county would have better sense than to even vote for me. I told her I didnt feel right takin their money. She said well you dont mean that and I told her I meant it ever word. We're six thousand dollars in debt over this job too and I dont know what I'm goin to do about that either. Well we just set there for a time. I didnt think it would upset her like it done. Finally I just said: Loretta, I cant do it no more. And she smiled and she said: You aim to quit while you're ahead? And I said no mam I just aim to quit. I aint ahead by a damn sight. I never will be.

One other thing and then I'll shut up. I would just as soon

that it hadnt of got told but they put it in the papers. I went up to Ozona and talked to the district attorney up there and they said I could talk to that Mexican's lawyer if I wanted and maybe testify at the trial but that was all they would do. Meanin that they wouldnt do nothin. So I wound up doin that and of course it didnt come to nothin and the old boy got the death penalty. So I went up to Huntsville to see him and here is what happened. I walked in there and set down and he of course knew who I was as he had seen me at the trial and all and he said: What did you bring me? And I said I didnt bring him nothin and he said well he thought I must of brung him somethin. Some candy or somethin. Said he figured I was sweet on him. I looked at the guard and the guard looked away. I looked at this man. Mexican, maybe thirty-five, forty year old. Spoke good english. I said to him that I didnt come up there to be insulted but I just wanted him to know that I done the best I could for him and that I was sorry because I didnt think he done it and he just rared back and laughed and he said: Where do they find somebody like you? Have they got you in diapers yet? I shot that son of a bitch right between the eyes and drug him back to his car by the hair of the head and set the car on fire and burned him to grease.

Well. These people can read you pretty good. If I had of smacked him in the mouth that guard would not of said word one. And he knew that. He knew that.

I seen that county prosecutor comin out of there and I knowed him just a little to talk to and we stopped and visited some. I didnt tell him what had happened but he knew about me tryin to help that man and he might could of put two and two together. I dont know. He didnt ask me nothin about him. Didnt ask me what I was doin up there or nothin. There's two kinds of people that dont ask a lot of questions. One is too dumb to and the other dont need to. I'll leave it to you to guess which one I figure him to be. He was just standin there in the hall with his briefcase. Like he had all the time in the world. He told me that when he got out of law school he had been a defense attorney for a while. He said it made his life too complicated. He didnt want to spend the rest of his life bein lied to on a daily basis just as a matter of course. I told him that a lawyer one time told me that in law school they try and teach you not to worry about right and wrong but just follow the law and I said I wasnt so sure about that. He thought about that and he nodded and he said that he pretty much had to agree with that lawyer. He said that if you dont follow the law right and wrong wont save you. Which I guess I can see the sense of. But it dont change the way I think. Finally I asked him if he knew who Mammon was. And he said: Mammon?

Yes. Mammon.

You mean like in God and Mammon?

Yessir.

Well, he said, I cant say as I do. I know it's in the bible. Is it the devil?

I dont know. I'm goin to look it up. I got a feelin I ought to know who it is.

He kindly smiled and he said: You sound like he might be getting ready to take up the spare bedroom.

Well, I said, that would be one concern. In any case I feel I need to familiarize myself with his habits.

He nodded. Kind of smiled. Then he did ask me a question. He said: This mystery man you think killed that trooper and burned him up in his car. What do you know about him?

I dont know nothin. I wish I did. Or I think I wish it.

Yeah.

He's pretty much a ghost.

Is he pretty much or is he one?

No, he's out there. I wish he wasnt. But he is.

He nodded. I guess if he was a ghost you wouldnt have to worry about him.

I said that was right, but I've thought about it since and I think the answer to his question is that when you encounter certain things in the world, the evidence for certain things, you realize that you have come upon somethin that you may very well not be equal to and I think that this is one of them things. When you've said that it's real and not just in your head I'm not all that sure what it is you have said.

Loretta did say one thing. She said somethin to the effect that it wasnt my fault and I said it was. And I had thought about that too. I told her that if you got a bad enough dog in your yard people will stay out of it. And they didnt.

When he got home she wasnt there but her car was. He walked out to the barn and her horse was gone. He started to go back to the house but then he stopped and he thought about her maybe being hurt and he went to the tackroom and got his saddle down and carried it out into the bay and whistled at his horse and watched his head come up over the stall door down at the end of the barn with his ears scissoring.

He rode out with the reins in one hand, patting the horse. He talked to the horse as he went. Feels good to be out, dont it. You know where they went? That's all right. Dont you worry about it. We'll find em.

Forty minutes later he saw her and stopped and sat the horse and watched. She was riding along a red dirt ridge to the south sitting with her hands crossed on the pommel, looking toward the last of the sun, the horse slogging slowly through the loose sandy dirt, the red stain of it following them in the still air. That's my heart yonder, he told the horse. It always was.

They rode together out to Warner's Well and dismounted

and sat under the cottonwoods while the horses grazed. Doves coming in to the tanks. Late in the year. We wont be seein them much longer.

She smiled. Late in the year, she said.

You hate it.

Leavin here?

Leavin here.

I'm all right.

Because of me though, aint it?

She smiled. Well, she said, past a certain age I dont guess there is any such thing as good change.

I guess we're in trouble then.

We'll be all right. I think I'm goin to like havin you home for dinner.

I like bein home any time.

I remember when Daddy retired Mama told him: I said for better or for worse but I didnt say nothin about lunch.

Bell smiled. I'll bet she wishes he could come home now.

I'll bet she does too. I'll bet I do, for that matter.

I shouldnt ought to of said that.

You didnt say nothin wrong.

You'd say that anyways.

That's my job.

Bell smiled. You wouldnt tell me if I was in the wrong?

Nope.

What if I wanted you to?

Tough.

He watched the little brindled desert doves come stooping in under the dull rose light. Is that true? he said.

Pretty much. Not altogether.

Is that a good idea?

Well, she said. Whatever it was I expect you'd get it figured out with no help from me. And if it was somethin we just disagreed about I reckon I'd get over it.

Where I might not.

She smiled and put her hand on his. Put it up, she said. It's nice just to be here.

Yes mam. It is indeed.

XII

I'll wake Loretta up just bein awake myself. Be layin there and she'll say my name. Like askin me if I'm there. Sometimes I'll go in the kitchen and get her a ginger ale and we'll set there in the dark. I wish I had her ease about things. The world I've seen has not made me a spiritual person. Not like her. She worries about me, too. I see it. I reckon I thought that because I was older and the man that she would learn from me and in many respects she has. But I know where the debt lies.

I think I know where we're headed. We're bein bought with our own money. And it aint just the drugs. There is fortunes bein accumulated out there that they dont nobody even know about. What do we think is goin to come of that money? Money that can buy whole countries. It done has. Can it buy this one? I dont think so. But it will put you in bed with people you ought not to be there with. It's not even a law enforcement problem. I doubt that it ever was. There's always been narcotics. But people dont just up and decide to dope theirselves for no reason. By the millions. I dont have no answer about that. In particular I dont have no answer to take heart from. I told a reporter here a while back—young girl, seemed nice *enough. She was just tryin to be a reporter. She said: Sheriff how come you to let crime get so out of hand in your county? Sounded like a fair question I reckon. Maybe it was a fair question. Anyway I told her, I said: It starts when you begin to overlook bad manners. Any time you quit hearin Sir and Mam the end is pretty much in sight. I told her, I said: It reaches into ever strata. You've heard about that aint you? Ever strata? You finally get into the sort of breakdown in mercantile ethics that leaves people settin around out in the desert dead in their vehicles and by then it's just too late.*

She give me kindly a funny look. So the last thing I told her, and maybe I shouldnt of said it, I told her that you cant have a dope business without dopers. A lot of em are well dressed and holdin down goodpayin jobs too. I said: You might even know some yourself.

The other thing is the old people, and I keep comin back to them. They look at me it's always a question. Years back I dont remember that. I dont remember it when I was sheriff back in the fifties. You see em and they dont even look confused. They just look crazy. That bothers me. It's like they woke up and they dont know how they got where they're at. Well, in a manner of speakin they dont.

At supper this evenin she told me she'd been readin St John. The Revelations. Any time I get to talkin about how things are she'll find somethin in the bible so I asked her if Revelations had anything to say about the shape things was takin and she said she'd let me know. I asked her if there was anything in

*there about green hair and nosebones and she said not in so
many words there wasnt. I dont know if that's a good sign or
not. Then she come around behind my chair and put her arms
around my neck and bit me on the ear. She's a very young
woman in a lot of ways. If I didnt have her I dont know what
I would have. Well, yes I do. You wouldnt need a box to put it
in, neither.*

It was a cold blustery day when he walked out of the courthouse for the last time. Some men could put their arms around a crying woman but it never felt natural to him. He walked down the steps and out the back door and got in his truck and sat there. He couldnt name the feeling. It was sadness but it was something else besides. And the something else besides was what had him sitting there instead of starting the truck. He'd felt like this before but not in a long time and when he said that, then he knew what it was. It was defeat. It was being beaten. More bitter to him than death. You need to get over that, he said. Then he started the truck.

XIII

Where you went out the back door of that house there was a stone water trough in the weeds by the side of the house. A galvanized pipe come off the roof and the trough stayed pretty much full and I remember stoppin there one time and squattin down and lookin at it and I got to thinkin about it. I dont know how long it had been there. A hundred years. Two hundred. You could see the chisel marks in the stone. It was hewed out of solid rock and it was about six foot long and maybe a foot and a half wide and about that deep. Just chiseled out of the rock. And I got to thinkin about the man that done that. That country had not had a time of peace much of any length at all that I knew of. I've read a little of the history of it since and I aint sure it ever had one. But this man had set down with a hammer and chisel and carved out a stone water trough to last ten thousand years. Why was that? What was it that he had faith in? It wasnt that nothin would change. Which is what you might think, I suppose. He had to know bettern that. I've thought about it a good deal. I thought about it after I left there with that house blown to pieces. I'm goin to say that water trough is there yet. It would of took somethin to move it, I can tell you that. So I think about him settin there with his hammer and his chisel, maybe just a hour or two after supper, I dont know. And I have to say that the only thing I can think is that there was some sort of promise in his heart. And I dont have no intentions of carvin a stone water trough. But I would like to be able to make that kind of promise. I think that's what I would like most of all.

The other thing is that I have not said much about my father and I know I have not done him justice. I've been older now than he ever was for almost twenty years so in a sense I'm lookin back at a younger man. He went on the road tradin horses when he was not much more than a boy. He told me the first time or two he got skinned pretty good but he learned. He said this trader one time he put his arm around him and he looked down at him and he told him, said: Son, I'm goin to trade with you like you didnt even have a horse. Point bein some people will actually tell you what it is they aim to do to you and whenever they do you might want to listen. That stuck with me. He knew about horses and he was good with em. I've seen him break a few and he knew what he was doin. Very easy on the horse. Talked to em a lot. He never broke nothin in me and I owe him more than I would of thought. As the world might look at it I suppose I was a better man. Bad as that sounds to say. Bad as that is to say. That has got to of been hard to live with. Let alone his daddy. He would never of made a lawman. He went to college I think two years but he never did finish. I've thought about him a lot less than I should of and I know that aint right neither. I had two dreams about him after he died. I dont remember the first one all that well but it was about meetin him in town somewheres and he give me some money and I think I lost it. But the second one it was like we was both back in older times and I was on horseback goin through the mountains of a night. Goin through this pass in the mountains. It was cold and there was snow on the ground and he rode past me and kept on goin. Never said nothin. He just rode on past and he had this blanket wrapped around him and he had his head down and when he rode past I seen he was carryin fire in a horn the way people used to do and I could see the horn from the light inside of it. About the color of the moon. And in the dream I knew that he was goin on ahead and that he was fixin to make a fire somewhere out there in all that dark and all that cold and I knew that whenever I got there he would be there. And then I woke up.

A-AR

MR A.S. ADAMS.

09-01-28

74146696

74146696